Melody

Happily Ever After

Melody
JEN MELLAND

Larkspur
KELSEY KILGORE

Evie
HILARY HAMBLIN

JEN MELLAND

HAPPILY EVER AFTER

BroadStreet
PUBLISHING

Melody

Broadstreet Publishing
2745 Chicory Road, Racine, WI 53403
Broadstreetpublishing.com

Published in partnership with **OakTara Publishers, www.oaktara.com**

Cover design by Yvonne Parks at www.pearcreative.ca
Cover and interior design © 2014 by OakTara Publishers
Cover images © thinkstockphotos.ca: Young woman smiling/Francesco Ridolfi, 159175680; Ocean, palm, paradise/kaliostro, 186992635
Author photo © Jennifer Melland

Melody, © 2014, Jennifer Melland; © 2013 as *Real Love,* by Jennifer Melland.

Scripture quotations are from the Amplified° Bible, © 1954, 1958, 1962, 1964, 1965, 1987 by The Lockman Foundation. Used by permission.

Sneak Peek *Larkspur,* © 2014, Kelsey Kilgore; ©2014, 2008 as *A Love for Larkspur,* by Kelsey Kilgore; author photo © Kelsey Kilgore.
Sneak Peek, *Evie,* © 2014, Hilary Hamblin; © 2014 as *The Arrangement,* by Hilary Hamblin; author photo © Hilary Hamblin.

ISBN-13: 978-1-4245-9904-2 ▪ ISBN-10: 1-4245-9904-0
eISBN-13: 978-1-4245-9905-9▪ eISBN-10: 1-4245-9905-9

Melody is a work of fiction. References to real people, events, establishments, organizations, or locales are intended only to provide a sense of authenticity and are used fictitiously. All other characters, incidents, and dialogue are drawn from the author's imagination. The perspective, opinions, and worldview represented by this book are those of the author and are not intended to be a reflection or endorsement of the publishers' views.

Printed in the U.S.A.

I am now a mere foot or so away from him, and his eyes are penetrating. Kaleidoscope eyes, as the Beatles' song says.

We stand there, staring at each other, the ocean set as the perfect backdrop behind us. I feel this ray of electricity connecting us. I know what this means, and I'm not sure if I'm ready for it....

1

"All my little plans and schemes
lost like some forgotten dream."

I'm flying. The sky is blue, the clouds are white, and the ground is, well, far away.

No, really, I'm flying.

Like in an airplane.

For the first time. Ever.

Pathetic? Yes.

Destination? Anything but pathetic.

So I am an author. Not really, but let's roll with it.

My name is Melody Rebekah Kennedy, and I am 19 years old.

And I've been addicted to alcohol for 12 years.

Okay, again, not really, but it so totally started out like an AA meeting.

To be serious, I actually have published a novel. Just this year, in fact, and this trip is what I rewarded myself with. Granted, I didn't earn all of the money, but I've also been saving for it since I was a kid. I think any girl needs to fly to the Caribbean before adulthood starts, don't you?

I started a book when I was 13 and finished it when I was 17. It was a cute book about a teenage girl going through the normal things, but she finally realizes that it's not her own life—and that there is a wonderful, amazing, and gracious Father looking out for her every move. Meanwhile, I underwent a similar revelation in my spiritual life—something I have no doubt God was involved in. He works in mysterious ways!

Okay, so you'd think an author like me would avoid run-on sentences in her head. But no, not me—I tend to talk a lot and put my foot in my mouth periodically.

Back to the beginning: so I wrote a book, miraculously had it published, decided to hop on a plane (which, again, I have never done before), and fly to Jamaica (JAMAICA!), to a somewhat private resort that my literary agent managed to get me a reservation in. But I am not alone on my journey.

Sitting next to me is Rosalyn O'Hara, my adorable best friend since grade school. Ros, as I affectionately call her, is reading a book (a vampire/werewolf romance novel—don't ask) and currently has her thick black-rimmed glasses pushed down to the very tip of her nose, so far down that I'm sure they will fall off if I nudge her ever so slightly…

I pull my hand back just as she jumps in her seat; my theory has been proven correct.

"Melody!" She turns to me, mock anger in her gaze.

I'm not the least bit worried. We both know how ridiculous she looks with her glasses on, not to mention when they slide down her nose instead of actually helping her see. Silly girl, she should just get contacts.

"Oh, you know it's a shame to hide those pretty green eyes of yours," I joke.

She wrinkles her nose.

Ros, like every other girl on the planet (including myself) has trouble realizing that she is beautiful. Her long strawberry blond hair dries perfectly straight without the use of any electrical devices whatsoever (and this totally makes me jealous because my hair,

2

equal in length, is dark brown with these crazy curls that frizz and stick out in no particular direction, and I couldn't straighten for the life of me).

Her light green eyes are mildly plain, but light up like crazy whenever she smiles, which is a lot. She has a contagious smile—one that has pulled me from the brink of depression numerous times. Plus, she's thin. I, on the other hand, have thick thighs, no butt, not so thin around the middle, and can barely fit into a bra that doesn't have *D* written on the tag. Okay, I understand that most girls consider large bra sizes to be an asset, but they don't work with the rest of my body. I'm lopsided! Not to mention the serious back problems that can cause.

Of course, this is an argument Ros and I have frequently:

Me: "You're skinnier and prettier than me."

Ros: "No way; you have a much better figure than me."

I love her to pieces, and there isn't another person I'd want to come with me to the beach for two weeks to do absolutely nothing but read a gigantic stack of books (which are supposed to "inspire" me). Oh, and tan, of course.

Basically, I just needed to get away.

I live in Washington—not D.C., but state of—which is totally boring yet incredibly cool. I don't think I could make it in the big city. I love the trees, the mountains, and the wilderness in general. I hate the snow (we get plenty of it), which is awesome because it's January and snowing at my house, but I won't be there to deal with it.

Ros has lived two blocks away from me forever but actually enjoys the snow. She snowboards. I tried once, and I will never, I repeat never, try it again. Ick.

I think we just flew through Colorado, our next stop being Dallas, Texas. I have never been there, and sadly, will only be there for about the 15 minutes it takes to walk across the airport and board the next flight to vacation land.

"You excited?" Ros can probably feel the waves of pure and simple joy emitting from my body, but she feels the need to ask the question anyway.

"Absolutely. I have never been…" I stop to think. "Anywhere. This is going to be great!"

Ros wrinkles her nose (a common facial expression). "Is Jamaica out of the country? It's only, like, 50 miles away from the coast, right?"

I smile. "It's closer to 600 or 700 miles, and no, it is not part of the United States. Therefore we are going out of the country."

Ros is sure pretty, and near perfect, but she doesn't necessarily have the highest IQ. She can get a little…odd…sometimes.

"Oh." She looks thoughtful. "So, like, is that a different continent?"

I burst out laughing, but then look into her eyes and can tell she's confused.

I sober slightly. I guess since I mentioned that I tend to be the smart one, I should act like it. "Oh, Ros, I love you. Jamaica is an island, but I don't know much of the historical background. It's warm and has sandy beaches. That's all I need to know!"

Ros nods in agreement, then sticks her nose back into her book. I can see her glasses start to slide back down again. I almost feel bad for laughing at her, but she knows me better than anyone. I am funny and sarcastic—both traits I get from my dad. I guess I can be pretty serious, because I wouldn't have been able to finish writing a novel if I wasn't. I love being a leader, and Ros is content with following. That's why we work so well together. I suppose I can be overbearing sometimes, but I'm a lot better than I used to be. I have learned to understand my flaws and improve them, thanks to God.

Which reminds me of the most important part of my life: I'm a Christian. Full-blown, born-again Christian. God has blessed me with my gift for writing, and I am terribly thankful to Him for that, among other things. I also am crazy about The Beatles and retro things. The three combined make for an interesting personality.

I blame my parents.

"Attention, passengers: We are now beginning our descent into the Dallas/Fort Worth airport. Please put your carry-on luggage below the seat in front of you. Also, fasten your seat belts and wait until the captain turns off the light," the head flight attendant warns us before I feel the plane slightly jilt. My stomach knots. I wasn't sick the whole flight, but the idea of us possibly crashing is slightly scary. I white-knuckle on Ros's knee, and she eyes me curiously.

"It's not my fault that I'm a plane virgin!" I say, probably a little too loudly, because a couple of people turn to look at me. I sure am glad we managed first-class seats for the way to Jamaica, because I wouldn't want to be packed any closer than we already are.

I peer out the windows as we slowly descend beneath the clouds. I start to see the patchwork quilt of land and soon buildings and even a river. Despite my imagination, we land safely and, surprisingly, on time. Ros and I grab our carry-on luggage and begin the walk to our next gate.

Okay, so for my first taste of Dallas, it isn't much. The people look the same as they did in the Seattle airport, except they all seem to be in a hurry to get somewhere. Nothing is really different about the atmosphere. It's even snowing outside, which is a huge disappointment to me. Ros seems disappointed, too. I didn't realize that it snowed in Texas, but this has been a weird year weather-wise already. Despite the snow, I can tell Dallas is extremely flat. I wouldn't want to live here for anything—the mountains keep me alive, I suppose.

We make it to our gate right as they start boarding our plane to Jamaica. Had we not caught this earlier flight, we would have been on the next flight out. Even with our later trip from Seattle, it would have been a four-hour-long layover.

We walk through a glass gate. "Good-bye, Dallas!" I whisper.

Ros follows suit. We board the plane with only one minor delay—some guy (a little cute, maybe) was sitting in my seat. I politely asked if that was 3B, and he apologized and relocated, not without casting a glance at the top of my shirt, which, from all the traveling, has managed to stretch and fall to a lower level than a modest Christian girl should let it.

He may be cute, but I glare at the guy as he gets in the seat behind me.

I gaze out the window and am suddenly overwhelmed with: 1) I will be flying over the ocean; 2) I am on my second plane flight; 3) I am on my way to Jamaica!

"How long is this flight?" Ros asks, looking pretty darn excited, too.

"I don't know…probably another three or four hours."

She remains quiet for a second, then swivels toward me. "Mel?"

"Yes?"

"Do you think there will be any cute guys there?"

I giggle. Despite her unbelievable looks and figure, Ros hasn't ever had the excitement of a boyfriend. Honestly, I've tried to talk her out of her wallowing, but she doesn't know yet that guys aren't all they are cut out to be. I'll let her live the experience, but not without a few warnings.

Obviously, my experience with guys has not been wonderful.

Growing up, I was a tomboy. All my best friends were guys, so I've been somewhat confident and comfortable around them my entire life. In middle school I had this guy friend I thought was wonderful. I even put him above Ros for a while. Then I developed a tiny little crush on him—not a big deal, right?

Wrong. Little crush turns into large crush, which turns into a lot of embarrassment and a loss of a good friend.

In high school I managed to crush on tons of guys, have dates to every dance, and never get seriously kissed…or asked for a second date. My mom has always told me it's because I intimidated them. Women are supposed to be submissive.

I understand that's what the Bible teaches, but I don't think God meant for women to lose their voices. And I am submissive to my parents and I will be to my future husband. But, while dating, I want to hold my own. I do not want to give the impression of passiveness to hormone-driven teenage males.

My first and only year of community college, I was pretty serious about this one guy. We never really dated, but it was more of a courtship thing because we were always with other people. We were about at the point where I was beginning to want to move forward when he got another girl pregnant. He was the church-going type. I learned that just because a guy says he's a Christian doesn't mean a thing. You have to watch for the proof in his life, or something bad could happen.

I notice that Ros has been staring at me for a few minutes while I had my flashback. I muster my strength to reply to her.

"Rosalyn O'Hara, we are going on a vacation, on a beach. It would be cruel not to have cute guys to stare at while we pretend to read." I say this, half convincing myself. Isn't that what I had hoped? That I would meet an amazing guy and have a summer fling? Maybe finally have a romance that would inspire me to write the romance novels I want to?

But aren't I a spontaneous individual who doesn't need any man to make me feel complete?

"Mel?" I realize I've drifted off again when Ros calls my name.

"Yes, Ros?"

"Thanks."

I know what she's talking about. Everything.

"You're welcome!" I grin back at her, diamonds playing in my eyes.

She reminds me of a Beatles' song.

7

Hot. Amazing. Beautiful.

And no, I'm not just describing myself.

I'm describing Jamaica.

The airport felt like a pool building, though. You know, the concrete walls, humid air? It only took a half hour for us to get through all the security procedures and get our passports stamped (yay!). My literary agent, Maggie, has been to this island a few times, and she arranged for us to stay at a huge luxury resort in Ocho Rios, which should be about a two-hour drive from the airport here in Montego Bay.

We're supposed to wait for someone from the resort to pick us up, but as Ros and I stand in the airport, we don't have any idea where to go. On my left, I see couples from around the globe being ushered into a waiting room that is specifically for Sandals Resorts. So maybe The Palm (our resort) has its own waiting room?

"Are you ladies lost?" A tall Jamaican man strides up to us, speaking surprisingly clear English from what I've heard on TV before.

"We're going to The Palm, and we're wondering where to go?"

"Yah, mon, to the right and keep going. You'll see the sign."

He points us in the right direction, and I thank him for his hospitality. Ros sends me an excited "squeal" look.

Sure enough, we round the corner, and after walking two minutes, we see a huge golden palm tree sign in the back right-hand corner of the airport. I quickly check us in. Ros may be good with people, but she can get confused, and I personally like to handle important details.

Soon we are ushered into a bus with about 10 others. There's one couple in back, but the rest seem to be singles like us. An intriguingly handsome guy takes the last open seat in front of us.

He smiles at us before going back to his book.

Ros leans forward in her seat to ask him a question. I can tell she's really going to pursue this whole "cute guy" thing. "So, how is it that it's snowing in Dallas and there is 90-degree weather here?"

I hit my head, wondering what would make her ask such a dumb question.

But he gazes back at her, confidence in his eyes. "For one, we're closer to the equator." He grins like she didn't say something totally stupid.

"Interesting. I never thought I'd be vacationing down here."

I'm slightly shocked at how easily Ros is opening up to a complete stranger. She does it at home…but here? What if we were to meet some psycho serial killer or something?

However, I only have a second to reflect, because then our bus starts moving. I guess the word *caravan* comes to mind. The speed limit is in kilometers, and I think that's smaller than miles, but I don't have any idea and the driver doesn't seem to notice the posted limit anyway. We follow a curved road out of the airport and don't even pause for a second before being slung into oncoming traffic. He veers to the left, speeding and following the car in front of us so close that if they slow down by the littlest bit, we'll end up hitting them.

Rosalyn falls back into her seat and grabs onto my hand for dear life. Despite the crazy driving and constant honking, she's soon lost back into her book. I shudder and peer out the window—reading in a situation like this would make me sick. To my left is the beautiful Caribbean ocean and so many resorts I lose count. To our right, a beautiful lush jungle splattered with ramshackle huts and loose chickens. I did not expect to see poverty night and day like this and immediately ask God for a way to help.

We stop halfway to get drinks and use the restroom, and Ros and I are startled at being offered a Red Stripe beer as soon as we step off the bus. Apparently, there's no drinking age in Jamaica. We both pass, but end up buying a cute sarong each at the gift shop.

Back on the bus, the populated area of Montego Bay slowly opens into beautiful countryside with vivid colors. The road widens, and there's suddenly less traffic.

It feels like forever, but we finally pull up to a set of golden gates. They're opened by an attendant, and we move forward to catch our first glimpse of our hotel. I hear Ros gasp. It's so extravagant—decorated in warm reds and oranges that remind you of the heat. You can see three, maybe four, blue pools lying on the grounds, and the cool part is that it is on the ocean (the beach is part of the courtyard)! It's busy, but not packed.

The driver becomes our bellhop and carries our luggage into the hotel lobby. "Misses Kennedy and O'Hara have arrived."

He actually announces us. I feel really special, and by the grin on Ros's face, she does, too. We are immediately checked in and shown to our room. The hotel has countless flours, with restaurants scattered throughout.

Our room is gorgeous. In the middle there is the living room and the kitchen, which we share. Then there is a small closet on each side, next to our bedrooms, which are huge with comfortable beds and bathrooms with Jacuzzis. It's a lot bigger and nicer than the apartment we share back home.

Yes, it may be pathetic to vacation with someone you live with every other normal day of the year. Oh well.

Ros and I both disappear into our respective bedrooms for a little nap and probably a shower afterwards. I haven't slept since leaving home at two in the morning…yesterday. It's almost evening here, so everyone recommends we sleep for the night and begin to explore in the morning. After all, we have two weeks—two long, glorious weeks.

My last thoughts before falling asleep: *Thank You, Jesus. I hope this trip is everything we've ever imagined, and I pray I might meet someone who will whisk my heart away.*

After a wonderful night's sleep, I wake at 6 a.m., Island time. I got more than 14 hours of sleep, which is amazingly crazy, seeing how Ros is still conked out. She could sleep through a hurricane.

I take a nice, long bath in my jetted tub and spend a little more time primping than I should have (just because I'll go swimming in a couple hours and ruin the look), then check on Ros. She's still sleeping, so I set out to explore.

The hotel recommends going anywhere you please inside of its grounds but also suggests that a young female doesn't go anywhere by herself. There's a small, somewhat Americanized town within walking distance.

With that caution in mind I begin exploring the lobby and the upstairs. I can tell already that Ros and I are way behind the rest of the guests by two or three social classes. I don't necessarily mean the money (but I'm sure that's true, as well) but more like the attitude—most of the people here get waited on hand and foot. Some, like Ros and me, love the attention but don't like putting another human being underneath ourselves.

We are also behind 100 percent on our attire. I just saw a man who was going out to play golf (yes, there is a golf course!) in a perfectly white suit. Whenever my dad plays golf, he usually comes back sweaty and maybe a little dirty. And our weather wouldn't be nearly this hot. Where's the practicality in that?

I stop and meander at a wooden rack filled with different activity brochures. After studying one, I find out there will be a dance two weeks from today. Interesting—a chance for Rosalyn and me to meet two fabulous fellows who will sweep us off our feet? Imagine the feeling, to truly fall in a deep, pure, real love....

My head is kind of in the clouds, which is why I'm not paying attention when I round the corner to go down the stairs. I don't normally ride the elevator if there are stairs, depending on the hike (obviously I don't want to walk down 50 stories, but one flight is perfect). Anyway, I turn and run right into some unsuspecting person carrying a lot of towels.

Not anymore. The towels, once perfectly folded, are now scattered around the hallway.

"Oh, I am so, so, so sorry!" I jump back, then immediately hit the ground and start trying to fold them back up. How did they do that? I stare at my rumpled mess, thinking they would look better if I had left them alone. I stand back up.

My victim catches my gaze, and these amazing crystallized eyes meet mine. They are green, but with so much gold in them that they glow. My eyes are sort of like that, but more plain and blue. His hair is brown, somewhat curly, and he's really tall. Like over six feet. I'm five-feet-five, so I'm stuck gazing up at him.

He stares into my eyes for a second. Not sure why, but I start to blush. He seems to notice and studies my face. He grins.

Wow. He was cute before he smiled, but now? My heart is beating fast.

"It's alright, no harm done. I was just taking these towels to be laundered." He speaks to me in a perfect British accent. I'm starting to think he looks a lot like Colin Farrell, British instead of Irish. Twenty something?

I ask the first question that comes to my mind. "If they were dirty, how come they're folded?" For a second, I feel like a complete idiot.

But then a crooked grin lights up his face. It's different than his regular smile—like he knows something you don't, and you're going to have to wrestle it out of him…really mischievous.

"I don't want to be carrying five unfolded messy towels around, do I?" He grins again. This time I notice how straight and white his teeth are.

It seems like hours that we stand there, staring at each other with these weird grins. I start to shift my feet. My heart is going a mile a minute, and his eyes never leave mine.

He's gorgeous.

It's time to leave before I start drooling or do something else equally embarrassing.

"I have to get back. Nice meeting you." I bolt out of his way and down the stairs.

By the time I get back to my room, I am hitting myself in the head. Why would I run away like that? He was so handsome!

Maybe…there might be a reason my heart was thumping so quickly.

2

*"Seems like all I really was doing
was waiting for you."*

I enter the room as Ros is walking out of her bedroom, toweling
her hair.

"Mel? I didn't even realize you had gone somewhere.
Exploring?"

I immediately relay the layout of the upstairs, the upcoming
dance, and the encounter with "towel guy" in the hallway. Ros
kindly bursts out laughing at my failure.

"Ros, don't you think it's weird? I prayed last night that I would
meet a guy, and I meet one today. Okay, so it was not in a
conventional manner, but I met one nonetheless."

She shrugs. "I don't know. You might not see him again, but on
the other hand, we are here for two weeks."

I stare off into space. "Yeah, maybe."

I still don't understand what caused me to run away from him
like that. What kind of girl am I? And if I just prayed about
wanting to meet someone, I totally ruined God's timing! But then,
even if I prayed for it, it only comes true if it's God's perfect will,
right? So I may not have totally screwed it up.

"I'm kinda hungry. How about you?" Rosalyn interrupts my thoughts.

I agree, so we head to the restaurant, making sure I'm paying attention as I round each and every corner. No sign of him, and now I'm really sad. What if Ros is right, and I don't see him again? He could be leaving today for all I know. That would certainly explain him taking towels back to the laundromat instead of waiting for room service to change them out.

We enter the restaurant and are immediately whisked away by the hostess and given two rather large menus. And they are just for breakfast!

"Wow," I say as I flip to the first page. "I didn't realize caviar was a breakfast food."

Ros looks awed. "They went all out, didn't they?"

It takes several minutes to survey the menu cover to cover, but Ros and I finally decide. The waitress, a tall, beautiful Jamaican lady name-tagged "Sophia," kindly offers to take our order.

"I'll have the Breakfast Extravaganza," I tell her. It really is extravagant! Hash browns, German pancakes with whipped cream and strawberries, eggs, bacon, and a glass of orange juice.

"How would you like your egg cooked?"

"Over-easy."

"Toast with that?"

"No, thank you." I never have been much of a toast-in-the-morning person.

"And for you?" She turns her attention to Ros, who basically doubles my meal except with her eggs scrambled.

After the waitress leaves, Ros raises her eyebrow at me. "So, mademoiselle, what is on the agenda for today?"

I laugh. "Do you even have to ask?"

"The beach!" we say in unison, something that happens a lot. I smile, knowing I've packed about four different swimsuits, complete with matching cover-ups and sandals, and I intend to buy more. A girl can never have too many swimsuits.

We finish our breakfast in silence, taking in the atmosphere. All of the Jamaican employees are dressed sophistically in black and white (my two favorite non-colors). The restaurant is decorated in almost an ocean theme, but not little-kiddish. More like the beach and bamboo—very elegant. It's how I imagine my future house to look, but with a husband and three-to-six kids.

I look over at Ros, who is staring aimlessly into space. Something in my heart pulls. I really wish she might meet a guy on this trip, just so she can know what it feels like. Nothing serious, because the odds of meeting a guy who meets all of her standards (very hard) on this island who would want to continue a relationship with a girl who probably lives hundreds of miles away is extremely slim. But a nice summer fling (well, January fling? It only seems like summer here) would be awesome to get her heart into shape for the multitudes of men who have crushed on her but never had a chance. She is really, really picky when it comes to guys.

I, on the other hand, tend to not think things through, which is why I have a slightly guarded heart and about 20 names attached to it. And, like I mentioned before, few even lasted past a first date (not always my decision). See, I have a theory, now that I've smartened up in the past couple of years. Looking back at all of my relationships, none have lasted more than two weeks (with the exception of my college boyfriend, who never actually dated me).

So, speaking as if the relationship is not going to work out, generally, I know a guy is probably not worth it by the end of the first or second date. That's when all of the pre-dating jitters begin to calm, and you start wondering why you were interested in him in the first place. By the end of the first week, you understand the relationship has nowhere to go and spend the next week trying to figure out how not to break his heart. If a guy can make it past those steps and past the two weeks without me wanting to dump him already, then I know he's a keeper. My older sister taught me this theory. There was only one guy who made it past the two weeks—my new brother-in-law! And she's only 20, barely a year older than me.

Some people say that it's crazy to marry young. I know my grandma has always told me to wait. But somehow, I've always felt that I would get married soon after high school. It's only been a year, but I already feel like my time is running out. I believe that with God, anything is possible, and if you truly love someone and pray about your future together, there's nothing wrong with getting married before you are even allowed to drink legally (at least in the state of Washington).

We leave the restaurant without having to pay a bill. The whole vacation, besides extra purchases, is all-expense paid, which is why it was pretty expensive in the first place.

Ros and I make it back to our room and are about to change into our swimsuits when we realize that it's only eight in the morning.

Our other option? Exploring!

"The town is within walking distance. Want to start there?"

Ros nods her agreement, and off we go. The grounds of the hotel are beautiful, lined with palm trees and beaches, and the town is just as pretty. It's touristy, with gift shops, coffee houses, and bookstores. Unlike the warm feel of the hotel, it has definite European influence. The streets are cobblestone, the buildings brick. It seems kind of weird for Jamaica, but I think the town was created because of the resort, not the other way around. There are hills that surround both the resort and the town, and past them is a forest filled with many different types of exotic trees and plants and animals.

Ros is so cutely intrigued with the whole place. She's always wanted to go to Europe and is planning a trip to France in the summer (the real summer). Our first stop is at the coffeehouse to get lattes. They have little scones and muffins, which we would buy if we weren't still completely full from breakfast.

"Can I help you with anything?" The woman behind the counter, I assume the owner, has a soft French accent. She's mildly plump, with short, graying hair. Come to think of it, she's the only Caucasian person I've seen here who hasn't been a guest. All of the resort staff has been native Jamaicans.

"Yes, what kind of coffee specials do you have?" I had looked around for a menu but didn't see one.

The woman rattles off about ten different drinks from memory. I decide on something that I suppose resembles a Caramel Macchiato from Starbucks. Ros, of course, goes for whatever has the most chocolate in it. Either way, our taste buds seem to enjoy the stuff. It's probably the best coffee I've had in a long time! Not too bitter, but not too sweet. We say good-bye to the lady and head off to the gift shop.

"Okay, so I need something for Mom, Dad, my sister, my brother, and Maggie." I list each person on one hand.

"Why don't we just look today?" Ros suggests. "We can save the actual buying until we're closer to leaving."

Ten minutes later I realize I made a mistake. Ros is the type of person who has to look at every single thing, in detail, while I only like to glance and stop at something of interest. Every two minutes she exclaims and starts talking about how cute this thing is or how old this piece is. Ros is in school for interior design, so she loves things that could be used in decorating.

Despite her comment to not buy anything, she ends up spending about 30 dollars on a few little trinkets.

I raise my eyebrows at her when we leave the store.

She glares. "What? They could be gone in two weeks!"

I smile. She's so adorable!

"Okay, but we are going to the swimsuit shop!" I lead her inside a cute store with hundreds of bikinis, tankinis, and one-piece suits.

I find a bright green suit to try on. At this point, I'm upset with God for making me bigger up top than most girls. The suit covers only the important part and leaves the rest open. But it's so adorable!

"Just buy it. You can always wear a tank over it," Ros suggests. It's weird, because Ros is a pastor's kid, but she tends to be a little more lenient about clothing. I don't like showing my body off, but she doesn't seem to have a problem with it. She says that if I have it, I might as well flaunt it. I'm not sure if I agree with her, but I buy the suit anyway. It's like she says—I can always wear a tank top over it.

It's lunch time when we get back to the hotel and drop off our purchases. We call up to the restaurant to order. Ros decides to go pick up the food instead of having room service bring it by.

I stretch out on the couch, thinking how nice it is to relax. I've always dreamed of coming to Jamaica, hence the reason I've been saving for a trip since I was little. When my royalties for my book came in, I stashed some in savings and pocketed the rest, ready to come on a beach adventure. Maggie has vacationed here many times, and since she's such a good customer at the resort, we managed to get a pretty decent discount. Plus, she let us steal some of her frequent flyer miles, so our expensive Jamaican vacation turned out to be moderately priced.

It's so exciting thinking about what's to come!

I'm nearly halfway asleep and starting to dream of the beach when I hear an excited squeal. I look up to see Rosalyn jumping frantically in front of my face.

"Mel, Mel, Mel, Mel, Mel!" she screeches.

I groggily wipe my eyes.

"What on earth?" Do I always have to be the mature one of the two of us?

"Melody, I met a guy!"

What? "Already? You were gone for ten minutes!" I sit up and turn my full attention on Rosalyn, who appears about to explode with happiness. *That was a quick prayer-come-true!*

"Yes, his name is Michael, and he wants me to come to the beach and play volleyball with him and some of his friends! Want to come?" She's so excited she can barely talk straight.

My mind, meanwhile, is battling. *Do I go to the beach? I hate volleyball. But Ros might need me there for support...or for protection. What kind of guy picks you up the first five minutes you meet him?*

"I'll come, but just watch the game." I reason, "Can we eat first?"

So we eat the second best meal of the day, even though I'm still mostly full from breakfast. After that we change into our swimsuits and cover-ups. I notice Ros is wearing her sexiest, tiniest bikini, without bothering with a cover-up. Something about it bugs me, but there's no way I'm going to say anything.

We walk only a couple minutes before we reach an area of the beach where a volleyball game is set up, and there are plenty of brown bodies from every nationality. Michael ends up being the typical surfer guy: tall, blond hair, blue eyes, big muscles, and not much of a brain. He and Ros are perfect for each other.

Okay, that was mean, and I know it, but I already don't have much of an opinion of the guy.

"Hey, baby. I knew you'd come!" He comes to greet us, and I step back, aghast. He called her *baby?* Already?!

Ros giggles like a little girl. "Mike, this is my friend Melody. She's going to watch the game, okay?"

Mike spends a second too long checking me out (or should I say my bra size?) before averting his gaze back to my smitten best friend. "Sweet. But make sure you sit far enough away. We tend to get a little rowdy." He addresses the comment to me but winks at

Ros.

He does this a lot. I can tell.

True to his word, the game starts going, and I have to move my beach towel farther away. There are a couple of cute guys, but none of real interest. I guess you can say that I'm a little picky about guys, too. It's not necessarily their looks, but I like to think that I can tell his personality right off of the bat, and that's what attracts me to him. Not to mention I'd already found the perfect guy.

I drown out the noise and stare at the ocean. I don't feel like going in the water, but it looks warm and inviting. I glance over at the game in time to see Mike "accidentally" run into Rosalyn, grabbing a full handful of her butt in the process.

Oh…my…gosh. I roll my eyes. I can tell Ros is totally into this guy, but I don't have to be a genius to see he's a creep. However, I also know Ros enough to know that I can't tell her this, or it will only drive her into his arms faster. But oh, how I wish I could!

Dear God, please let Ros be okay….

I decide I'll let her make her own mistakes, but I'll interfere if I think she's in any sort of danger. She may be smitten, but she's smart enough not to do anything she'll regret. I hope.

Meanwhile, my mind is taking turns back to this morning and a certain young British gentleman. I keep glancing around the beach, wondering if he's here. He seemed so…mysterious. Does tall, dark, and handsome ring a bell in anyone else's head?

Who is he?

And why do I see his face every time I close my eyes?

After about three hours of me half-sleeping and watching the game, Ros jogs over to me. Her grin is unmistakable.

Uh oh.

"Mike wants to go to dinner. You don't mind, do you? I mean, you weren't expecting to do everything together on this trip, right?"

She says it really fast, not even looking at me. I follow her gaze to Mike, who has taken off his shirt and is standing with his guy friends, probably planning his next move to get her into his hotel room.

And her comment stings a little. Actually, I did expect to do almost everything together. That was kind of the point, right? But oh well. I wave my hand as if it's no big deal. "Have fun."

"Great! See you tonight." She starts to walk away but turns back. "Oh, I don't know how late I'll be. Mike says they offer movies in the recreational center at night."

With that, she's gone, without a care and without another glance at me.

I'm the individual of us both, right? I can take care of myself.

But I don't really think I like being alone.

And, judging by the warmth on my skin, I'm probably already sunburned.

Just peachy.

I spend the next six hours flopped out on my huge bed reading the biography of John Lennon. Mostly I am into fiction, but I love Lennon. I actually cry thinking of the day he died (my mom does, too), and I wasn't even alive yet.

What saddens, and slightly worries me, is that it is 9 p.m., and Rosalyn is nowhere to be seen. She left for dinner at 3.

Now I totally understand that I seem like a mom right now, but I can't help it. It's like letting this pure, innocent little girl walk right into a nest of vultures (do vultures have nests anyway?) and just standing there watching.

I could prevent it. I could warn her. But would it help? She would probably start running instead of simply walking.

I start to cry and fret and pace the room when I hear the front door slam. It's more like 10 now. I run out to the living room, only to come face to face with a joyous Ros.

"Oh, my goodness, Melody! I had the most incredible evening. He took me out to dinner and acted like a complete gentleman. We walked hand in hand along those cobblestone streets in town. He walked me back here to our room." Ros takes a deep breath. "And he kissed me!" She doesn't seem to notice that my face is red and blotchy and that I'm wringing my hands.

My mind is saying, *Uh oh,* but I force myself to smile, hoping my worry is not evident. She finally got her first kiss, huh? I can't take back any of my pointless kisses, but I wish she had held out for a hero, not some tan muscle guy who only wants to get her in bed. She deserves better.

Then I let my "best friend" persona win out over the "mom" one.

"Oh, Ros, tell me all about him!" I know how to keep her happy, so basically we change into our pajamas and go into her bedroom and talk for the next several hours.

Ros goes over every detail, avoiding the fact that I personally saw him feeling her up, more than once, in front of all his friends. A girl deserves a little more respect than that, don't you think?

My heart's not in it.

But do I really, truly think I'm better than Ros? Because I know that we're both God's little girls, and we're completely equal. And while she seems to be abandoning her morals in exchange for romance, I'm sitting here begging and praying for God to send me a guy.

I don't know what to say.

3

*"Just like little girls and boys
playing with their little toys."*

Ros is gone when I wake up.

There is a scribbled note on the kitchen counter that reads: *Went out with Mike—don't know when I'll be back—have a nice day!*

Great. Alone again.

God, I know I prayed for her to meet a guy, but I didn't want it to be at the expense of me!

I realize my prayer was totally contradictory. I guess her meeting a guy in two weeks would probably mean that she would spend less time with me. But it's only our third day here (second and a half, but whatever) and I am already alone, bored, and almost out of options. I can't go anywhere beyond the hotel alone (I suppose I can, but I don't think I'll risk it); therefore, I am stuck on the beach. Might as well get excited about it.

I honestly think I'm still full from my two meals yesterday, so I take a shower and decide to simply walk the beach. It's only crowded right in front of the hotel.

I stroll along the surf line, noticing that, despite the warm weather, plenty of clouds threaten to cover up the sun. The water is body temperature, and I don't bother wearing flip-flops. I heard somewhere that sand is the best natural exfoliate. If that's the case, I am also receiving a wonderful spa treatment.

They have scuba diving, but you have to take a class; snorkeling, but I wouldn't want to do that alone; hiking—again, wouldn't want to do that alone; jet skiing, but not so exciting alone...so I keep walking.

There isn't much I can do here alone. The thought provokes a Beatles' song, and I start singing "Eleanor Rigby": "All the lonely people...where do they all come from?"

I am about 100 yards down the beach when one of those clouds, which has suddenly become a lot darker than it was a minute ago, lets out a sprinkle.

I brush it off. It's warm. Who cares if it rains a little?

But within two minutes, that sprinkle has turned into a downpour. I search for cover, realizing for the first time that each hotel room faces the ocean and has a covered patio, including ours. I feel stupid, like with the vacation my IQ is dropping by the second.

I run to one that resembles mine (although they all look exactly the same), and sure enough, the room number is also on the outside of the door, as well as a card slot for the passkey to go through. I'm about to go inside when I notice how pretty the rain is, now that I'm no longer in it.

The beach is now deserted. The clouds aren't everywhere, and there's this one beam of sunlight that seems to escape, making a rainbow. It also transforms all those little raindrops into crystals floating in the sky.

It's breathtaking.

I wish I had a camera.

I am basically relaxed, staring at the magnificent sight before me, when I hear a clear, strong voice singing one simple line:

"Lucy in the sky with diamonds…"

More amazingly, the voice almost sounds like Lennon.

It sings a couple more lines of the song, and I'm brought out of my relaxation and begin scanning for the culprit. His voice is rich and smooth, and I'm magnetized to it. (Picture me walking with zombie arms outstretched, my eyes rolled back into my head.)

Each patio is covered overhead and on the side, so you can't see the next patio. The voice is coming from the right, so I inch toward the wall, peek over, and—I gasp.

It's towel guy! I start panicking. What do I do? Any second, he's going to notice me watching him, and he's probably going to flip out and think I'm stalking him, but I promise I'm not, and wow, is he adorable!

Okay, so I make a decision. I want to see him, but not like this.

I'm about to duck away when he turns and looks at me.

I am caught. Red handed.

Again.

Towel guy appears awfully confused for a second. Then recognition pops into his eyes.

He remembers me! Despite the embarrassing circumstances, my heart jumps.

What is it with this guy that makes me want to pop down on my knees and kiss his feet? Keep in mind that's only an example.

"It's you. Trying to sneak up on me again, are you?" He directs the question to me, that crooked grin stretching ear to ear. He doesn't look a bit creeped out, thank goodness.

I'm about to answer when I stop to think how ridiculous I must look peeking around at him. I step off my patio and into the sand so he can see all of me, not only a select portion of my head.

Then I remember that I'm soaked head to toe, probably with little bits of mascara running down my face.

Oh, boy. I step down from my perch and walk onto the sand so we can actually see each other.

It's still raining.

"I heard you singing." I focus on my toes, thoroughly at a loss for words.

You don't know me very well yet, but you probably can guess that doesn't happen a lot.

"The Beatles' song, right? You might not know who Lucy was or why I was singing about diamonds," he admits carefully, sizing me up.

"Actually," I smile my best coy smile, "the Beatles are my favorite band. Secondly, I was just thinking myself that the raindrops look like crystals, so I figured that you thought they looked like diamonds, and that's why you chose that particular song to sing. But at that point, I didn't really know it was...you...singing, and I only wanted to see who that voice belonged to."

He appears shocked at my admission.

The hallelujah chorus is sounding in my ears. *I've impressed him!*

He sobers, then nods toward the beach. "I think it's the coolest thing when it rains here. There's almost always some sunlight, so it makes the rain seem less depressing than in most places. Did you see the rainbow?"

"Yes." We stand there in silence, watching the rain. It's not stopping, and I am still standing in it. I fidget. He seems to notice that I'm getting even more drenched than I was to begin with.

"Sorry. Would you like to step under my covering?" he offers, and I gladly step out of the rain, no matter how beautiful it is.

It also means that I am now a mere foot or so away from him, and his eyes are penetrating. Kaleidoscope eyes, as the Beatles' song says.

We stand there, staring at each other, and I feel this ray of electricity connecting us. I know what this means, and I'm not sure if I'm ready for it. Romance? It's not that bad of a thing, seeing how I've never really been romanced before, but I don't know if I can do it for only two weeks without coming away broken-hearted. But I did pray about it, and this is the second time I've met him, so maybe I should just…let go.

But can I do that?

"By the way, I'm Jude."

Jude.

His eyes don't leave mine for a second. It almost unnerves me, because it feels like he can see all the way to my soul. A jolt runs down my spine, and I shiver.

"Oh, you're freezing! Want to come inside? I'll get you a towel."

I'm glad he assumes it's because I'm cold. He all but pushes me inside his room. Normally I would be freaked out, but for some reason, I have this impression that he is harmless.

Jude disappears into what I can assume is the bathroom in search of a clean towel, leaving me standing awkwardly and soaking wet on his carpet. After seeing him with all of the dirty towels yesterday, I don't know if he even has one. His room is identical to mine, and I notice there's a second bedroom. Hmmm.

He emerges with not one, but two clean towels. The first one he hands to me; the second he spreads on the couch and motions for me to sit down.

I do, and he joins me.

But he doesn't say a word…only sits there staring in front of him.

This is really awkward. I'm actually starting to memorize the wall before he turns toward me expectantly. "Are you going to tell me?"

I look at him, bewildered. *What on earth is he talking about?*

"Your name, Miss…are you going to tell me your name?"

Oh. "Melody."

"Nice to meet you, Melody. You look like you've had an interesting day." He doesn't make a move, and it's weird. Throughout our introductions, he hasn't even made a move to shake my hand, which is the complete opposite of Michael and Ros.

I take a minute to size him up. Yup, definitely a young Colin. His brown hair is curly, but also kind of long on his face. He has a stubble on his chin that I'm sure was left there on purpose. And those eyes...they're wonderful.

I can tell he's sizing me up too, but not in a sexual way, and I have to admit, it makes me blush. And it feels really...nice.

The words of "All You Need Is Love" are circling throughout my brain, making it into one big mushy love pit. *"Love, love...love is all you need...."*

Jude is still gazing at me, and I blush again. *Maybe you should say something, Melody!*

"Yes," I answer, "I have had an interesting day. I started to go for a walk when this happened." I gesture to my clothes that are starting to dry.

Jude smiles and motions to the beach. The rain has stopped, and the sun once again warms the sky.

"Would you like to finish your walk, perhaps with some company?"

Hmmm...do I really need to think about my decision?

"Yes," I answer, possibly too quickly, but Jude doesn't seem to notice. He's smiling at me. *Oh...my...goodness.*

I've been talking a lot more to myself in the last hour than in my entire life.

Jude and I reach the beach and head in the same direction that I started in earlier.

"The rainstorms...are they common?" I ask, assuming he's either been here before or knows a little more about Jamaican weather. Anything to hear that accent of his!

"Yes, this is my second time at the resort, and it never ceases to amaze me how quickly they come and go."

We fall into step together, the only sound the waves crashing against our feet.

"So, Melody, tell me about yourself." He seems genuinely interested, unlike a lot of guys who merely fake interest to get what they want.

I like him already.

I blush. "What would you like to know?"

He regards me with this soft expression. I can't quite read it, but it makes my heart flutter. "Anything. Everything. What makes you unique?"

"Okay, in a nutshell: I love to write with a passion. I have been making up stories and imagining them on paper for as long as I can remember. It's a gift. I love black and white, classic things, retro things, polka dots, and The Beatles." I smile as he laughs with a rich baritone. "What about you?"

It's his turn to blush slightly. "Well, I grew up to The Beatles, so I must say that I love their music. Actually, they are my inspiration. I love to sing, and I play the guitar. Music is my gift. If you don't mind me asking, why do you say that writing is your gift?"

I hesitate. This is the part where I tell him that I am a Christian. Usually a few things can happen: he looks shocked and vows never to talk to me again; he simply nods but vows not to let me too close; or he gets excited and admits he's a Christian too. The latter hardly ever happens. Never, in fact, that I can remember, except for the guy I met at church who didn't seem to know what believing in Christ really meant. Therefore, I choose my words carefully.

"I believe each person is given a gift by God, but it is up to them whether they choose to use their gift to glorify the Lord." I say it in a way that he can understand my beliefs without seeming like I'm pushing them on him.

He seems to pause for a minute, and I start to think how stupid I am, when Jude breaks out in a breathtaking smile. Something tells me that the last scenario is true. *Thank You, Jesus.*

Jude looks equally thrilled and thankful. "Well, Miss Melody, I thank you for your frankness in your answer. I find subtle bluntness to be an art, and you seem to possess that quality. I too believe that God has given us each a gift. I pray that you use yours to the best of your ability."

"You're a Christian then?" I ask, hoping to get the answer in the open. Just because people believe in God doesn't mean they live their life according to His Word. But something tells me…

"Yes, I am. I have fully given God my life, and although I have my struggles, I like to think that I live my life according to Him. I'm greatly surprised and relieved to know you are a Christian as well." He smiles, again looking straight into my eyes.

I can't take it again, so I avert his gaze to my feet. He's going to make me fall in love with him, and fast.

"Where did you grow up?" I ask, trying to take the conversation into another direction. It almost scares me how comfortable I am with Jude already, especially now that I have learned of his faith. *It's a God thing.*

"Liverpool, England. I walked the same streets that The Beatles did; I grew up in the same area. Penny Lane." He stops. "How is it that you came to love The Beatles so much? They aren't exactly the most popular band in this day and age, especially for girls."

I laugh, mostly because he's right. "My mom. I blame her completely. Both my parents are into classic rock and oldies, but Mom would always play Beatles' songs when we cleaned the house. I remember dancing into the living room to 'Free As a Bird,' my mom crying. I have to say, I inherited her love for the music."

Jude nods. "I firmly believe that in order to appreciate where music is today, you have to appreciate, if not enjoy, where music came from."

"And The Beatles basically shaped the rock and roll music we listen to, even Christian music."

Jude looks nervous, almost scared for a minute before he smiles again. *Weird.* "I know a lot of Christian bands that state The Beatles as their main musical inspirations, and I don't blame them."

I get all warm and fuzzy inside. This means not only is Jude a Christian, but he actually listens to Christian music, not only mainstream. I like to balance both. Honestly, the lyrics in Christian music are great, while the actual music and talent are questionable. It's the opposite with classic rock and oldies—the music itself is phenomenal and talented, but the lyrics are questionable.

I'm glowing. We have so much in common!

"Okay, so where did you grow up, Miss Melody?" he asks. Most of my friends call me Mel, but for some reason, I love my full name coming off of his lips. Miss Melody sounds so…respectful, almost, like he appreciates the woman inside of me. And I honestly think he does, even though he doesn't know me. Perhaps he is just a gentleman.

"Born and raised in Washington State in a little town about 100 miles outside of Seattle. We don't have a lot of famous people who came from our state, but we are famous for coffee!"

He chuckles. "And you are a coffee drinker, then?"

"Yes, do you drink tea?"

Jude makes a sour face. "I can't stand the stuff! I hate it that the British are known for their tea. We can make a mean pot of coffee as well."

It's my turn to laugh. "I like iced tea, with a lot of sugar, but besides that, I agree with you."

I look over at Jude almost admirably as we walk the next several minutes in silence.

I can't even begin to comprehend what's happening here. Jude is probably the greatest guy I have ever met, and I'll only get to see him for two weeks.

A terrible pang of sadness overwhelms me. Would God bring him into my life, then rip him away again?

Jude seems to notice my change in attitude. He stops, then pivots to face me. The surf is brushing against our feet.

"Miss Melody?" he whispers in a hopelessly romantic voice.

Darn accent.

I lift my chin to face him. "Yes?"

"Why are you so sad all of a sudden?"

We stand there, facing each other, with the ocean set as the perfect backdrop behind us. The blue-green waves crashing are the only other noise I can hear besides my heart beating. I consider my options for a moment. I decide to come out with my feelings. Worst thing is that I'll scare him away and won't have to worry about leaving after all.

I shift my feet before answering. "I was thinking that you are wonderful and amazing, and I've only known you for two hours. And it's horrible because I leave on the first of February, and I'll probably never see you again. I was wondering what purpose God had in mind for us meeting."

There. I said it.

Again Jude remains quiet long enough for me to start to regret my words. Then, "Melody," he says carefully, "I don't know what God's purpose is, but we must trust that by the end of our time together, He will reveal it to us. I too am saddened when I think of leaving. I was thinking how silly it was right before you told me your feelings. It's like God is with us in every step that we take, even though it's only been a few hours since I met you. But you know what's neat about all this?"

"What?" I am greatly distracted by the pools of green staring straight through my eyes and into my soul. *Again.*

"I'm here until the first as well."

Yes, it's only been a few hours, but right now I decide not to dwell on what I am leaving, but rather on what may already be developing between Jude and me, because it seems like something that may last a long time.

And, for once in my life, I am content with following God's leading in regards to my heart.

It feels...amazing.

4

*"Seems like all they really were doing
was waiting for you."*

I am pretty excited about telling Ros all about my fabulous day,
but she hasn't shown up back at the room yet. It's two in the
morning.

At this point, I haven't seen, nor heard from her except for her
note *yesterday* morning. After my walk with Jude on the beach, it
was late afternoon. He invited me out, but I declined because I
thought Ros would be here, wondering where I was.

She isn't.

I don't know Mike's last name or how to contact him. I don't
even know if he is staying at the hotel. He could be some runaway
from a secluded Jamaican asylum.

Breathe, Melody!

Okay, that may be overreacting, because Mike doesn't seem like
the kind of person who has the brain capacity to even figure out
how to kidnap somebody. But then again, it could all be an act.

Mostly, I am worried about Mike pushing Rosalyn too far. Ros
kind of lets people push her around. She's extremely passive. It
works in our relationship, but with a jock like Mike, he probably
has had plenty of practice of talking girls into going to bed with

37

him.

When it's nearly 3 a.m., I have the phone in my hand to call security when Rosalyn walks in. Her hair is messy and her lipstick well worn off.

She says "hi" and acts completely innocent.

Calm down, I tell myself. *It's no big deal.*

I blow up. "Where the heck have you been?!" I nearly run the 10 feet between us, my hands in the air.

She looks scared. "Whoa, Mel, slow down. Are you okay?" She heads into her bedroom.

I follow. "Am I okay? What about you? I was so scared, Ros. I thought you had been kidnapped and raped! I was about to call hotel security to start searching for you!"

"I'm here now, so chill." She starts taking off her jewelry and brushing her hair.

I take a step back. "Were you with Mike?"

Ros looks at the floor, then back up at me. "Yes."

"What were you doing?" I pursue.

She looks guilty, and then a sudden anger flares in her eyes. "You know what, Melody? It doesn't matter what I was doing. You are not my mother! I don't have a curfew, and it is not your job to take care of me. I am sick and tired of you pushing me around."

I take a deep breath. It's pretty unlike Ros to get mad, especially to yell at me. I can tell there is a new development in her personality, no doubt from hanging out with Mike and his friends. Still, I know I shouldn't push my luck.

"Sorry, Ros, I was just worried about you. You're right. I am not your mother, and I don't have a right to baby-sit you. However, I thought we'd taken this vacation to spend time together."

She opens her mouth to protest, but I continue calmly, "Now that our plans have changed, I at least want to know a time period to expect you and where I might be able to contact you in case something comes up. I came back for dinner without realizing that you had other plans. Can we coordinate our schedules a little better next time?"

Ros looks me straight in the eyes, and I can tell there's something she wants to say. But she doesn't.

"Fine," she spits out bitterly.

Then she walks into her bathroom and slams the door.

Wow.

Now I am in serious need of some beauty sleep.

Somehow, though, between dreaming of a really hot British guy, and fretting over my fight with Ros, I doubt that's going to happen.

God, please protect Ros. I want her to be safe, but I don't want her to feel like I am mothering her. And I pray you guide my relationship with Jude, whatever it is. Amen.

Surprisingly, Rosalyn is still at the room when I get up the next morning at eleven. But she actually turns away when she sees me. Talk about a cold shoulder!

"I thought you'd be gone," I say, plopping down on a plush chair.

"Mike had to work," she says quietly.

Yes, that does explain a lot. He must work at the resort or something. I want to ask, but I don't.

"Oh." I can tell she's still a little peeved at me from the night before. I also know, keeping our few previous fights in mind, that it's probably better to let her stew for a while before approaching her about the subject again, no matter how much I want to talk to her about things.

"What are you doing?" she asks.

Good. She's starting to make peace!

I am about to answer her when the room phone rings. It's on the table next to me. "Hello?"

"Melody?" A distinct British accent greets me.

I break out into a huge grin, and it's obvious Ros is completely confused. We told our family only to contact us through email unless it's an emergency, and as far as she knows, I haven't met anyone else.

"Hey."

"It's great to hear your voice." He nearly whispers the words in that romantic voice of his, causing a huge blush to cover my face.

"It's great to hear yours, too." I wince at how lame the conversation is, at least on my part.

Luckily, Jude gets straight to the point. "I have plans for us this afternoon and evening, but like any good gentleman, I would like to run them by you first for approval. And, of course, in case you have anything planned already with your friend?"

"Thank you for the consideration." I glance at Ros. No way do I want to spend a day with that glare. "What did you have in mind?"

"Well, it all starts with a picnic on the beach…"

Jude explains his plans, and we agree to meet on the beach at two. I hang up, and Ros is staring at me with her eyebrows raised.

"Ummm, I met someone," I explain. She almost, almost, looks excited for me. "I'm meeting him at two, and then we're going to stay up past sundown because he has the perfect star-watching place in mind."

Ros appears amused. "So it's okay for you to stay up all night with a guy?"

"Rosalyn, is Michael a Christian?" I'm blunt.

She seems surprised, then flustered. "Yes. Well, I don't know, but I guess he is." She thinks for a minute. "Okay, maybe not. No, he isn't."

I nod knowingly. "Jude is. To me, it makes all the difference in the world."

Ros seems to listen but still disappears into her room. I walk to the patio doors and open the shade, relieved to see not a single cloud mars the horizon.

Excitement fills the space left hollow by Ros's resentment. I rush to eat a small breakfast (because I have to leave room for my picnic!). By the time I take a shower and try on about every bathing suit/coordinate outfit in my closet, it's nearly two o'clock.

"Ros?" I knock on her bedroom door. Without replying, she opens it. I can tell that she's been reading, and I know what happens to Ros when you interrupt her. Let's just say that you need to make whatever you have to say really fast.

"I wanted to let you know that I'm leaving. I will probably be back by midnight, but it's best not to expect me, okay?"

She nods, surveying my outfit. I had decided to wear my new green bikini, only because I had brought a cute green sundress with Hawaiian flowers that looked great over it.

"I forgot you brought that dress." Ros almost compliments me.

"Me too."

She looks uncomfortable. "I might be hanging out with Mike tonight, but I should be back around the same time as you."

"Okay." I start to walk away but turn around after a few steps. "Ros?"

"Yeah?"

"I love you."

A meek smile lifts the corners of her mouth. "I love you too, Mel."

I meet Jude next door. He's packing the rest of the picnic basket and I'm walking around his room. I glance at the kitchen table and am extremely surprised to see a copy of my book.

"Jude? Are you staying here alone?"

"No, actually, I'm on a family vacation. My sister, Beth, is staying in the second room and our parents got a suite a few floors up."

I motion to the book. "I didn't think you'd be reading a teen romance, but I wanted to make sure." I smile, but my heart is doing back flips.

"Me? No. And I try to talk Beth out of them too. Those books are nothing but fairytales that trick young girls into thinking men are decent and love is easy."

I gape.

Jude smiles apologetically. "I'm sorry. I know you like to read. But some of those romance books are poison."

"It's okay, no big deal." I smile, and we head out onto the beach to a little cove Jude picked out. We're asking each other questions, and I'm trying hard not to dwell on what just happened.

"Okay, favorite movie?" It's my turn to ask a question.

He looks thoughtful. "I don't really have one. I enjoy many of the movies that I've seen, but none enough to call my favorite."

"I completely agree with you on that one. And to be honest, it surprises me…"

"…how much we have in common?" He finishes my sentence.

Great. One more thing to add to my growing list of things I love about Jude.

"Yes." I look out to where the waves crash in the ocean. It's amazing here, and spending the time with Jude makes it so much more fun and romantic.

"It's uncanny, isn't it?" He pauses, then leans in closer. "I have to be honest with you, Melody. Ever since yesterday, I have been praying my heart out to God, but I have this unbelievable sense of comfort about our friendship."

Oh, crap.

I sigh. There it is: the *F* word. It's the word every girl hates to

42

hear at the beginning of a relationship, and I've heard that word more times than I would like to admit.

*Friendship, just friends...*what a romance killer!

Jude doesn't seem to notice my change in attitude this time. He's staring out at the ocean, watching it move with life. There's never a dull moment.

"Have you been swimming yet?" he asks thoughtfully.

"Not yet. I was going to swim yesterday, but you know how that turned out."

He smiles, as if the memory warms his heart. All I can think about is how horrible I looked when I saw my reflection in the mirror after our day together. I was really surprised he wanted to spend time with me again today.

"Well, what do you say about getting wet on purpose this time?" he asks as if he had been reading my thoughts. He stands and offers his hand to me. Jude then strips off his tank top and jean shorts (don't worry, he has swim trunks on underneath), revealing chiseled abs, tanned to perfection.

I actually gasp.

And sit back.

I have to force myself to breathe.

Wow.

That is one of God's beautiful creations!

Now I am suddenly concerned. I wore my new bikini without thinking—all I have on is the dress to cover it up. I look very cute in it, but it's probably not the most modest thing in the world. I feel like I should issue a warning to him, but he's already running down into the water. I slowly grab the bottom of the dress and lift it over my head. I nervously adjust the suit, trying to make it cover more than the fabric will actually allow. I turn toward the ocean, and that's when I see Jude.

He's standing there, up to his waist in water, staring at me with his mouth open. I walk cautiously toward him, barely feeling the warm water hit my body.

"Sorry, I know it isn't that modest of a suit, but it was just meant to be worn under the dress. I didn't realize we'd be swimming. I should have brought something. Sorry," I babble.

Jude shakes his head, as if waking from a trance. "Don't be sorry. You're beautiful." His expression melts. It almost feels like he's going to kiss me.

I lean forward, waiting for his touch…

Wait.

Jude pulls back. "It's just going to make things a little harder, that's all. But I can handle it."

Wow.

I am relieved…and sad at the same time. Why didn't I want Jude to kiss me?

What girl wouldn't want a romantic kiss in the ocean?

Wait. The voice inside my heart was adamant. *Wait.*

Okay, but now Jude and I are staring at each other awkwardly.

He wanted to kiss me, I know it.

I dunk into the water, amazed by how awesome it feels to swim. I can see the sand through the blue-green water, rippled perfectly from the waves.

"They offer snorkeling here, you know. It's free," Jude offers, seeming to understand my admiration at God's creation. Luckily, the awkward moment has passed, but only barely.

I shake my head. "Maybe tomorrow. It's nothing like the water I am used to. I've swum in a couple of lakes that I'd be afraid to see what's on the bottom!"

He looks shocked. "Haven't you ever swum in the ocean before?"

I shake my head as I do a shallow dive. "It's too cold to swim on the Washington coast."

Jude and I swim in silence, not going too far away from our spot on the beach. He has a good backstroke.

Oh, my goodness, Melody Rebekah, what are you doing? You're complimenting his backstroke in your head, and HE ALMOST JUST KISSED YOU.

He almost just kissed me.

I almost let him.

And I'm glad I didn't.

But why?

After almost an hour, the pruning of my hands drives me back onto the shore.

"It's time for some serious tanning," I say as I collapse on our blanket. Chuckling, Jude follows suit. I gladly get settled, momentarily forgetting I'm half naked in front of a completely fabulous guy.

"Melody?" he asks thoughtfully after several minutes.

"Yes, Jude?" I roll over onto my back.

I vow, silently, as of right now, to never wear this bathing suit again, outside of a tanning bed. It causes too many lustful thoughts…from both of us.

"Do you like poetry?"

I smile. "I love it. I started writing poetry before I realized that my talent went beyond that. Even got one published in a magazine when I was 13."

"Really? Can you recite it for me?" He sounds genuinely interested. I'm glad he likes poetry. That's usually a good indication that a guy is either gay or romantic, and I'm thinking the romantic part fits him.

I squint up into the sun, trying to remember the poem. I start slowly. "Have you ever been to that place, with gleaming white snow, and shining, golden roads? Have you ever heard that sound, soft as feathers, but as loud as loud? Have you ever seen that sight, been blinded by that wonderful, sparkling, bright light? Have you ever smelled that smell that tickles your nose, the aroma much sweeter than a rose? And have you ever felt that way that makes you so joyful, that you always want to stay? I have, every day."

I look at Jude for his reaction. He's thinking.

"It's about heaven, isn't it?"

I nod. "It's actually the title."

"Wow." *He liked it! He really liked it!* "If your poetry was that good at age 13, I can imagine how creative your novels must be today."

I almost tell him the reason I'm in Jamaica is because I got a novel published, the one he'd said bad things about. But something inside me keeps those words from coming out. If our relationship progresses, I might tell him, but not now. I don't want to ruin what we have. So I answer simply, "Thanks," even though I'm beaming inside.

The sun eventually dries us off, and then Jude suggests we have a sandcastle making competition. We spend nearly an hour, occasionally throwing sand at each other. He wins by a long shot. My castle is a little mound of sand that falls to pieces every second.

"Now, how is it we decided I have the creativity and the imagination, but your sandcastle is the amazing one?" I snap my fingers. "Right. I lack the artistic ability."

"Oh, don't cut yourself short." He sits next to me. "See, if you built a tower here," he uses both hands to make a combination of dry and wet sand to create a tall tower, "and make a moat like this…it protects your castle from the waves."

Halfway through his moat making, a large wave crashes up and destroys my castle. I start laughing hysterically.

Jude smiles. "Okay, maybe not."

Of course, now we're covered in sand, so we have to swim again. I think, hopefully, Jude has gotten used to the sight of me in a bikini. He no longer stares at me with drool dripping down his chin. Part of me wishes he did.

After drying off again, I put my sundress back on. It's already evening, and I'm starting to get hungry. And a little chilly.

"How long until sundown?" I ask, trying to cover up the growls my stomach is making.

He hears my pain and pulls out some snacks for dinner.

Wow. Jude's some kind of amazing, isn't he?

"Only about 15 minutes. It's the one side effect of this island having great weather. The sun goes down fairly early."

I nod. Sure enough, moments later, Jude and I watch the sun descend behind the horizon.

"Welcome to the Caribbean, love," he quotes.

I pretend not to notice the fact that, while he was quoting Johnny Depp, he called me "love."

"It's beautiful." Oranges, reds, purples, and pinks blend together to make one big artistic canvas, and it feels like it is only inches from my fingertips.

"Yes, it is," Jude answers.

I turn to look at him, but realize he isn't even looking at the sunset. He's looking straight at me. It seems like something out of a romance movie. I blush like I have never blushed before, but I don't think he can tell because of the dark shadows on my face.

Did I mention that this feels a little too good to be true?

"Do you have a girlfriend?" I blurt out, completely ruining whatever opportunity there might have been for romance.

He looks shocked. Poor Jude. "Do you honestly think I would be spending time with you if I did?"

I shrug, feeling foolish. "You said we were friends."

"We are, Miss Melody." His eyes meet mine with intensity. "Every potential relationship needs to have a strong foundation in friendship. No, I do not have a girlfriend. Do you have a boyfriend?"

"No."

"Why are you here?" he asks.

Without revealing my book, it takes me a minute to come up with a reason. "To relax with my best friend before facing the challenges of life and college." I manage to explain my reasons without lying or giving too much information.

"And have you?"

"I've managed to drive her away in four short days." I explain to him about Ros meeting Mike and my worries about the two of them. "I realize she's her own person, but she's never gotten her heart broken. I don't want to see it happen, especially if they get physical. The fact that she looks almost guilty when I see her makes me think the worst."

"I suppose you are bothering her a bit." I begin to protest, but Jude senses it. "Don't get mad, Melody. It's like when a mother keeps telling her child that a stove is hot. The kid doesn't believe her until he touches it. Then it's too late; he's already been burned. But you can bet that he will never touch a stove again."

"Thanks." It's incredible that he's able to explain all of my feelings with one little analogy I already knew.

"What are you and your family doing here? Besides vacationing?"

"I needed to get away from life, and they decided to come with me. I've got a big decision to make about something, and we were hoping the Caribbean sky would help."

The stars are starting to appear in the now dark sky. Jude and I lay next to each other, watching them. I can tell he's in a total spiritual zone, so I remain silent.

God, You are doing something totally amazing in my life. I saw the bad effect of Mike on Ros, but I hope others can see the good effect of Jude on me. I feel calmer, less juvenile than I did a mere four days ago. My excitement seems more...relaxed. If anything, I can tell You already had a purpose for bringing Jude into my life.

I hope he can say the same thing about me. I hope I am leaving an impact on him in a way that will stay with him forever, even if I won't be able to.

And, Lord, please help him with whatever decision he needs to make. I pray that I can be a solid support. I also pray that one day soon he will trust me enough to share his secret with me. Amen.

5

*"Don't need to be alone.
No need to be alone."*

I wake up the next morning calmly, feeling refreshed and rejuvenated.

And cold.

I try to move, but my back is fairly stiff.

I put my hands down on my bed to lift me up, but they just sink.

They sink in *sand*.

My eyes fly open, and I am greeted with the ocean.

Oh, crap.

I rub my face, trying to figure things out.

Jude is right beside me, sleeping soundly.

Oh, crap.

Judging by the placement of the sun, it's about six in the morning. We fell asleep on the beach.

Oh, crap.

"Jude," I whisper. No movement.

"Jude." I say it this time a little louder.

"JUDE!" This time I give him a slight push.

Fidgeting, he opens his eyes. He smiles the most adorable smile

I have seen on a male. Ever. It lights up his face and gives me butterflies. "Melody, I was just dreaming of you," he murmurs, taking that sexy accent to the extreme.

I can't help but blush. "Um, Jude?" I look around, trying to get him to notice where we are.

It takes him a minute, but his eyes widen. "Oh, my goodness, Melody!" He shoots up into a straight position.

I have to get back to the hotel. Pronto.

"Sorry, Jude, I have to go." I grab my sandals in my hand and take off running in the sand.

I don't know if you've ever run in the sand, but it's not easy. Especially not barefoot, two minutes after you wake up.

Nevertheless, I make it back to my hotel in record time. I open the slider door with the passkey, only to reveal Ros with bloodshot eyes. She isn't smiling.

I don't know what to say, and excuses run through my head a mile a minute. I feel like a little kid who got caught taking a cookie out of the jar when she knew she wasn't supposed to.

"Do you think this is funny?" she asks, gritting her teeth. I don't think I have ever seen Ros like this, and it scares the heck out of me.

"What? No, Ros, you don't understand!" I try to explain, but she's made up her mind.

"Is this some sort of payback for me staying out the other night? Huh?" She takes a couple more angry steps toward me.

"Ros, no, it's not. I am so sorry, please believe me."

Ros crosses her arms. *Prove it*, her look says.

"Honest. Jude and I were looking at the stars. It was so peaceful and…we must have fallen asleep because I just woke up five minutes ago…and I ran all the way here and…" I take a deep breath. "I'm sorry."

Tears started streaming down her face. "I know I should be so mad at you like you were to me the other night, but Mel, you scared me so bad. When you didn't come home at all, and I didn't know where Jude's room was, it made me realize how scared you must have been for me, so I spent half the night feeling horrible for being so mean to you, and the other half freaking out because I didn't know where you were."

I lead her to the couch, where we both sit quietly. "Thanks. And I really am sorry."

She gives me a huge hug. "I guess I wasn't too scared. You are a lot stronger than I am. I was mostly afraid that you were only doing it to get back at me. I was worried that if I had made you that mad…"

Ros is interrupted by a light knock on the sliding door.

"Jude." I get up to open it, letting him inside.

"Melody, I'm so sorry." He seems to notice Ros and directs his apologies to her. "I promise we fell asleep and we…we didn't do anything. And she ran here as soon as we woke up—"

Ros smiles. "I understand. I'm really relieved she's home now."

"And nice to meet you, Rosalyn. I have heard so much about you."

I smile at his unbelievable manners. There's the gentleman I know!

Ros looks surprised I've been talking about her. I send her a return glance that says, "Of course, Rosalyn, you are my *best* friend in the whole wide world!"

Jude nods to her, and I offer to walk him out.

"I think I should spend some time with Rosalyn today. No matter how weird it was to wake up on the beach today, at least Ros is speaking to me now."

"Melody—" He is clearly at odds for what to say.

"I'll call you, okay?" I send him a smile that I hope carries my words.

He smiles, seeming to understand that we (as in Jude and I) are still okay and that I am not mad, and then he excuses himself to his side of the patio.

"I didn't realize that his room is right next door." Ros is standing right behind me in the doorway. I can tell from her expression that she watched the whole thing, including the very tender gaze Jude gave me before he left.

"It's how we met. Well, for the second time." I smile nervously. Ros seems better, but I don't want our friendship to be at stake because of a couple of guys.

Her eyebrows lift, this time in a good way. "You mean Jude is towel guy?"

I nod. *Good. Ros is happy.*

"Wow, I have to hear this story!"

This time, we crash on *my* bed and listen to *my* guy story. I relate the past couple days to her, including the little voice that keeps telling me to wait.

"Mel, that's amazing." She looks away. "I have to admit, it sounds a lot more pure than the relationship I have with Mike."

"Have you…" I hope I don't have to finish the sentence. I love her and don't want to embarrass her.

"No. *No.* But he's tried. I mean, I like him, but I think I realized sometime last night that I need to be more careful. I admit the fact that I knew you were with Jude, who's a Christian, helped calm my spirit. I was able to pray for the first time in a few days." She appears sad, but happy at the same time.

"And I apologize for overreacting. I could kind of tell that Mike was just in it for the physical stuff, so that made me extra worried," I admit to her, finally.

"You did? How did you know?" She eyes me warily, like I'm about to tell her I'm psychic.

"The first day on the beach when you were playing volleyball, he tried to touch you every chance he got." I shrug. "It's something you'll notice once the first relationship is over, especially if it's like this one."

Ros frowns as if she's perplexed. "You know, thinking back, no wonder you didn't seem excited about me meeting a guy. I thought you weren't happy for me, but really you saw something in him that I didn't." She stopped. "But you let me make my own mistake."

I nod. "You never would have learned otherwise." I tell her about Jude's analogy on the beach. I probably make him sound much smarter and more reasoned that it really was, but I've realized I have a rather biased opinion of him.

Darn that accent!

I think about the rest of the trip. We're on the fifth day, already. I remember dreaming about how long and relaxing this vacation was going to be. Instead, it's been one emotional rollercoaster after another. But I have to stop and consider Ros in the fact that I can't last the next week without Jude by my side. It's simply not possible.

"I don't want to make you feel left out by me hanging out with Jude. I'm sure he's perfectly willing to include you, but I don't want you to feel like you're a third wheel," I reason, hopefully giving her the hint that, even though she's welcome, I would rather get in whatever time Jude and I might have together before we go our separate ways.

Rosalyn doesn't look the least bit left out. Instead, she's blushing. "Um, I met someone else, besides Mike. Sort of."

"What? You little player!" I hit her with a pillow. "Why didn't you say something?"

"It's the guy from the bus here, Mel. I mean, he showed interest in me, but I was paying too much attention to Mike to notice. His name is Jason, and he's a Christian. We had some time to talk last night. I went to meet Mike at the bonfire, but he never showed up."

What a creep! Mike stood her up? No wonder she freaked out about me not coming home. She had already been jilted by one person last night.

There is one tiny, little, miniscule…okay, it's a huge part of me…that is extremely glad Mike finally proved who he really is before he had the chance to take the most important thing away from my best friend.

Thank You! The angels are watching!

An idea is forming in my head.

It's great!

It's amazing!

It's the talk of the year!

Okay, maybe not, but you'll understand soon enough.

I grin slyly at Ros. "Do you have his room number?"

She nods, obviously wondering what I'm thinking.

I smile. "I told Jude I wanted to hang out with you today, but I have the perfect idea for tomorrow night…."

It's already been an exhausting day, but Ros and I rent chick flicks and crash on the couch with chocolate.

Okay, she's eating chocolate. I like the stuff, especially dark, but I have never taken to it as my comfort food. It's just not good to me in large quantities. I snack on a carrot for one of the first times in my life.

"Isn't he just the hottest?" Ros sighs longingly at the screen in the middle of *Sweet Home Alabama.* She's talking about Ethan Embry.

"Amazingly. But why did he have to play a gay guy in this movie?"

"You know, he looks like him." She's still staring at the screen. This time, there is something different in her eyes.

"Who?" I am really confused. Ethan Embry looks like…Ethan Embry. Right?

"Jason."

Oh. I get it.

"You know who Jude looks like?" I ask her. She barely saw him for a minute, but I'm sure Rosalyn caught the resemblance of my latest romantic interest and the Irish bad boy.

"Colin."

She catches my eye, and we break into a hilarious fit of giggles.

Girls will be girls.

"Do you think Jason is ready for a real date between you two? I know you mentioned you met him, but are you comfortable with him yet?" I cooked up this idea of having Jude and Jason over for a little dinner party tomorrow night. We called both of the guys already to see if they had any previous engagements.

They're coming.

"Yes. He has already asked me out. Twice."

"And you said no?" I ask incredulously. Jason has already asked Ros out? Jude hasn't even touched me yet!

She nods sadly. "I was too busy daydreaming of Mike. I'm sure Jason feels like a rebound guy, but he did agree to come. I even told him to dress up. There's something about him...."

I know that look. It's the "la-la land" look. I'm sure I've had the same expression four, maybe five times already today, while thinking of Jude.

She breaks the look off. "Mel, I think whatever you have with Jude is going to turn into something special, something to remember. I don't know what it is, but I have this gut feeling..."

It's my turn to nod vigorously. "I have the same feeling. Jude and I were talking about what possible reason God could have for putting us together and tearing us apart. I was praying that night, and I actually think Jude is helping me mature into a better person. Does that make sense?"

"Completely. I can see the difference. You seem calmer, more at ease. Like you said, older."

I don't mention to her that I'd noticed Mike was starting to turn her into a reckless jerk. Let's just sweep that one under the carpet. "Do you think you and Jason will last beyond the vacation?"

"No. I think God might have sent him to show me that not every guy is a jerk like Mike. Unless something extraordinary happens in the next week or so, I doubt we will even write to each other."

Her words get to me. Already I am dreading leaving Jude, and there's not a single chance I would leave without his promise to write. *"I don't want to fall asleep, 'cause I'd miss you, babe, and I don't want to miss a thing…even when I dream of you, the sweetest dream would never do, because I'll miss you, babe, and I don't want to miss a thing."* Choppy lyrics to an Aerosmith song play through my head. My feelings for Jude are becoming obvious in my mind, but I'm fighting them.

Have I already fallen for him?

Yes.

Plain and simple.

But the question is: what do I do now?

6

*"From this moment on I know
exactly where my life will go."*

"Okay, so they just delivered the food, right? I can smell the Chinese!" I hollered out my bedroom door. Ros and I had opted to go for a more Oriental dinner versus the steak and salad we'd originally planned. We both had a huge craving for Sesame Chicken, my favorite dish.

"Yeah, but Mel? Can you come here?"

I walk out of the room wearing just my underwear. I've been staring in the closet for about 20 minutes and still haven't chosen between the three nice dresses I brought along.

Ros doesn't even flinch when she sees me. How completely sad is that?

She's standing over the table, which she so nicely set and decorated, holding a lighter as far away from her body as humanly possible.

I giggle.

I forgot—Ros is deathly afraid of fire, or at least smart enough not to trust herself with the flame. I light the candle, and she seems to notice that I'm nearly butt naked in our living room.

She stares at me thoughtfully. "I like the blue dress."

"Okay, then I'll wear the blue dress." I head back into my room to dress.

See, simple as that!

It only takes a minute to slip into the dress.

I swish in front of a full-length mirror. Ros is right. The blue sets off my eyes.

I walk out into the living room to see that Rosalyn has changed in the same exact time as I have. She's wearing a white dress in almost the same T-style.

Together, we are unstoppable!

(Insert evil laugh.)

"You know, I don't think Jude has ever seen me with makeup on. I was drenched with my mascara running down my face."

Yeah. It's definitely not one of my prouder moments, thank you very much.

She snickers. "You're going to knock him dead, Mel."

We stand side by side, appraising ourselves in the hall mirror. We look good.

I glance at the clock. "It's time."

We stand around, seeing how the food is already spread on the counter, ready to be served, the table is set, the candles are lit, and the music is playing (soft oldies, thanks to the hotel collection). All that we are missing is the guys!

At that moment, there are two simultaneous knocks—one from the slider, one from the front door.

Punctual, aren't they?

I grin. Widely.

I take the slider; Ros heads for the door.

"Hi," I greet Jude as I open the door for him.

"Oh. Um, wow. Melody, hello."

I giggle softly. His expression of admiration rivals the one he had on the beach when I stripped down to my bikini. This one makes me feel a lot more beautiful, though.

"Welcome to our humble abode." I walk him into the living room, where Ros introduces a slightly uncomfortable looking Jason.

She's right. He does resemble Ethan Embry.

"Please, gentlemen, sit." Ros and I pull out their chairs, implying for them to sit. I can tell Jude is not used to sitting before a woman at a dinner, because he nervously shifts his gaze. Jason doesn't look like he's feeling very well. Poor guy is crazy nervous! But someone with Rosalyn's beauty has a tendency to have that effect on men. She never notices it.

Ros and I take in their outfits with appreciation. Both are wearing black slacks, white shirts, and ties. Completely adorable.

"Darn, Mel, Jude looks sexy," Ros hisses in my ear as she passes to get the sparkling cider out of the fridge.

"Jason's not too bad himself," I whisper back.

Within moments, we are all seated. Ros and I exchange silent glances.

I clear my throat. "Jude, would you like to bless our meal?"

He seems pleased that we asked him and looks a lot more comfortable than he has all night. "Father God, thanks so much for our fellowship tonight, and bless Rosalyn and Melody for ordering this wonderful meal for Jason and me. I thank You for allowing us all to meet, and I pray that the next days will be fulfilling toward our lives. In Jesus Christ, amen."

There's a lump in my throat.

By golly, I think I may have found me a godly man.

I discreetly wipe the tears from the corners of my eyes. Jude catches me and sends me a mix of the crooked, mischievous grin and the gentle, sexy smile.

The butterflies in my stomach are now doing aerobic exercise.

It's at this point that I am pretty confident.

He likes me.

He *really* likes me.

He stares into my eyes during the appetizer, during dinner, and during dessert, all the while managing to maintain a more than polite conversation with the other two people at the table.

Wait, there's more people here than just Jude and me?

You could have fooled me!

The evening continues without a hitch. Jude and Jason hit it off and soon are having a deep conversation about Christian music in England. I didn't even realize there was Christian music in England.

And how does Jason know about it? He's barely said a word all night, but I don't think the guy is British.

Ros and I retire to the patio, leaving the guys to talk on the couch. I snuggle up beside her and put my arm on her shoulder. I'm so glad we are back to normal. In fact, I think these past couple of days has made us stronger.

"Best friends forever, right, Ros?" I hold my wine glass filled with sparkling cider out in front of me.

"And shall we never let a guy between us again." She lifts hers to mine to make a soft *clink*.

We giggle like second graders. Pulling apart, we are both lost in our own train of thought. I'm sure hers involves Mike and Jason. I'm thankful I hadn't blown my top before I did, because I don't think Ros would have made the quick recovery from Mike. I know he's called the room a few times, because I'm the one who has answered the phone.

Ros is over him, thank goodness, and much more relaxed in her relationship with Jason. He seems a lot more timid than Mike has probably ever been in his life, and that makes me, the motherly type, a lot more comfortable.

I turn to look at Jude through the door. He's the only thing I've been able to think of all day. I see his face every time I close my eyes.

"He hasn't touched me," I admit to Ros. I told her about Jude being seemingly pure before, but I didn't elaborate.

Rosalyn lifts a brow. "Not even a hug?"

I shake my head. "He came about two inches away from kissing me the other day at the beach but pulled away at the last second. We slept side by side, but he never laid a hand on me." I smile. "Well, unless you count me running into him in the hallway."

Ros is silent. Then, "Wow."

"I know." I feel the same way—awed by him, by God, and by how our relationship is progressing.

I can't stop staring at him. The lamp light is catching his hair so that it appears nearly golden. His dancing green eyes are animated as he talks to Jason, but he stops, turns toward me, and grins an award-winning smile.

He felt my gaze.

My heart soars.

Ros catches the moment. "Jude is special to you, isn't he, Melody?"

I can barely muster the strength to nod. "You've known me all my life, Ros. This feeling is…greater, more powerful, and way more…adult…than anything I have ever felt. And it's been a week." I realize my words as they are out of my mouth. "It's been a week," I repeat.

Ros knows the meaning: the two-week theory.

"So, at this point in the relationship, the original feelings should start wearing off and you should be wondering what you see in him, right? Or is it that you know the relationship has nowhere to go, and you have to figure out a way to leave without breaking his heart?"

"Right," I whisper, and then smile at Ros.

She looks beautiful tonight, and I pray that God sends her someone special soon, maybe Jason, just like God has sent me Jude.

God sent me Jude.

Forever, my little voice says. *Forever.*

7

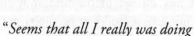

*"Seems that all I really was doing
was waiting for love."*

That's the first thing I wake up to the next morning.

God sent me Jude.

Forever.

The idea is still dancing in my head, making exquisite figure eights.

The problem is that I don't know if my heart is simply saying those things, or if God did indeed send me Jude.

Okay, well, I admit Jude is in my life for a reason, but that reason may not be forever.

Right?

And I couldn't possibly be in love with him.

Right?

I mean, it's impossible. I've known him for a week.

Right?

It's about this point where I start freaking out.

I have known Jude for a week, which means this vacation is half over. This means I only have one more week to spend with him. Less than a week, actually: five days.

And I was supposed to be relaxing on this trip! I pull myself out of bed. It's time for some serious girl talk.

I walk out into the living room wearing an oversized T-shirt.

"Ros, I need to talk to you." I spot someone on the couch, but it isn't Ros.

It's the person who occupied my dreams last night.

And the night before.

And the night before that.

Well, you get the point.

"Jude!" I yelp, pulling my T-shirt down so it covers my legs.

He laughs at me, instead of running away like I thought he might. Wow, I look like a fool! But he meets my eyes and avoids the fact that I'm half naked. Then I realize I'm better dressed than when I was wearing that green bikini.

"Rosalyn is off with Jason. She let me in only a minute ago with permission to raid your refrigerator of last night's leftovers."

"Oh. Well, I'll be right back." I run into my bathroom to pull on a pair of shorts and make an attempt to brush my hair, but end up just throwing it into a scrunchie.

I don't look amazing, but it'll do.

I'm back in the living room in record time. Even Jude seems impressed.

He gets his hot, crooked grin. "So what do you think about snorkeling?"

"Snorkeling sounds…wonderful."

Anything I do with you sounds wonderful.

The "look" of snorkeling is not wonderful. There's a mask involved that covers my face and makes me feel like I'm about to suffocate.

Enough said.

But the really cool thing is that Jude doesn't even seem to care.

Well, I guess he can't because he has one on, too.

And his is bigger, so he looks even goofier than I do.

Back to the point: there's this awesome pier that I didn't know existed off of the other corner of the beach (the one we started to explore). There's also a waterfall somewhere up there too, but we didn't walk that far.

Instead, we rented snorkeling material. Jude, who has gone before, gave me a quick tutorial. We probably aren't doing it 100 percent correctly, but it's okay because we still get the effect of it.

It's weird, though, because you have to breathe through your mouth; otherwise you will kind of choke.

It's worth it.

And it's beautiful.

You can see every little thing underneath the water. I don't like the idea of seeing the fish, but they are fascinating. And I have to admit I probably would not have tried snorkeling if it wasn't for Jude. He has a knack for getting me to do new, fun, and exciting things.

And Jude himself is new, fun, and exciting.

Believe it or not, though, I'm swimming here, looking underneath the water, and I'm not really thinking of Jude. Instead I'm thinking how great and magnificent God is to have created all of these things. How intricate the details are, and how He put everything together perfectly. He even put me together perfectly.

He put me with Jude….perfectly.

Okay, so maybe I am thinking about Jude, but only a little bit.

It's kind of hard not to when he's right beside me.

I turn to see his hands in the water, but they're not there.

He's not on the other side, either.

Then I see a dark shadow out of the corner of my eye. Definitely not Jude.

I tear my mask off. "Jude!" I start to panic, thinking there is probably a shark or something equally scary only a couple feet from me.

Luckily, Jude's head pops up about 20 feet away. "Melody, are you okay?"

I scan around me, seeing no signs of anything dangerous.

And I start to realize that I totally flipped out and that I'm really embarrassed. "Um, can we head back?"

I see his grin. "Sure."

So we start swimming back. This time I feel Jude's arm hit me every few minutes.

This time, instead of thinking, I enjoy myself.

And it might only have a little bit to do with the fact that Jude is right beside me like a comforting force.

We're lounging on the beach, drying off.

"What do you want to do now? Swimming? Jet skis?" Jude asks, obviously excited about the action-packed, fun-filled day he has in mind for us.

I squint out to the water, thinking of the scary, dark shadows I'd seen. "Um, maybe we can, you know, stay…away…from the water," I say nervously.

Jude starts laughing hysterically. "Melody, you really were afraid out there, weren't you?"

I can tell he's slightly concerned, but the choking laughter that bubbles out of his throat overwhelms that.

I roll my eyes. "I just want to do something without getting wet again, okay?" I might be a little defensive, but he totally deserves it.

Jerk.

But at the same time, I'm not the least bit mad at him.

Odd, right?

He finally manages to stop laughing. "Okay, well, we can just walk…on the beach…like we always do."

Okay, so he's right. There's not much to do here that doesn't involve water sports, unless he wants to play golf, and I am totally against that. Sorry. It's the one sport I don't like. But now I'm feeling bad because I'm ruining this perfect day and…

So I take off running down the beach, my feet splashing in the shallow water. I'm the one laughing because it takes Jude a good minute or two to realize what I'm doing.

But he figures it out and starts chasing me.

Now, I may be a little heavy, but I'm not out of shape. It's just my bone structure. *Really.*

But Jude is fast compared to me, like super-duper fast. Within two seconds he has caught up with me, even though I had a good two-minute lead on him. Instead of tackling me, which is what I'd assumed he would do, Jude simply jogs beside me all the way back to the hotel. It's nice, but I'm at the point where I can't really breathe anymore.

Luckily, we're at the back of his hotel room. Exhausted, I collapse onto the warm sand.

Jude does the same.

And now we're sitting here, out of breath.

"Wow. I haven't run that fast and that long for a while," he admits.

"It felt good. I know I'm not in the best shape." I'm sure my hair is windblown, my face is red, and I feel pretty sweaty.

Jude brushes away a curl from his forehead. "Who are you trying to fool, Miss Melody? You look gorgeous."

If Jude has made me blush before, it was nothing like the red that is on my face now. I'm sure I must resemble a tomato, but he is giving me a look he's never given me before, no matter how many sexy smiles he has blessed me with.

His curls are untamed and everywhere; his face is slightly pink. His eyebrows are raised, revealing forehead wrinkles that are there before their time. His eyes, green and shining, are locked on mine.

He's staring at me, but there's something different in his eyes.

Jude is looking at me like he loves me.

And it's scary as all heck.

Because I love Jude back.

"It won't be long…till I belong to you…"

"Oh, Ros, what am I going to do?" We are stretched out on our couch with our sliding glass door open to the sunset. The sun is gorgeous.

"What makes you think that you have to do anything about it?" she asks, paying more attention to her lack of a manicure than to my words.

"How can I not do anything? Jude has fallen in love with me, Rosalyn."

This time, she looks up. "Yes, it's quite obvious Jude is in love with you, Mel. And it's just as obvious that you love him back. So what's wrong with that?"

I stand and start to pace. "Because we are both leaving in less than a week and we might never see each other again. He's quite possibly the most amazing guy I've met in my entire life, and I'm going to be impossibly broken-hearted."

She's staring at me, and it's making me nervous.

"What?"

"Mel, where's your faith?"

Faith.

Right.

I look at her. Maybe she's smarter than I've been giving her credit for. But is it really possible that I am in love with Jude? After only a week?

"Do you believe in love at first sight? Yes, I'm certain that it happens all the time!" I hear the words of The Beatles in my heart.

Ros sighs, then rolls off the couch. "Oh, Mel, there's another bonfire tomorrow night. Jason and I are going. Would you and Jude like to join us? We are going to sing around the fire. It's mostly a group of Christian kids."

I shrug, preoccupied. "I'll ask Jude, but I don't think we have anything planned."

"Good, let me know." She walks out of the room, probably to read one of her vampire novels she's so into.

I'm alone with myself, and I have to say it's a scary thought. I walk out to the patio and gaze up into the sky. *God, what am I going to do?*

"I know, Charles, but I'm working on it. I think I've made my decision." I hear Jude's distinct voice on the other side of the patio. "It's...well...I've met someone. Yes, she's a Christian. No, she isn't famous." He sighs. "It won't be bad for publicity; I don't even want publicity. I've got to go; I'll call you tomorrow, alright?"

Okay, I know this could constitute as snooping, but what is Jude talking about? Publicity? Hmmm...

I'm considering walking over and surprising him when he moves out onto the beach. He doesn't even go a couple hundred feet before falling down on his knees. He looks...confused.

No matter how curious I am, I'm sure he will tell me when the timing is right. For now, I'm going to pray for him, because that's the only thing I know how to do.

I sneak quietly back into the room and fall asleep on my bed, wondering what God might have in mind for my future.

8

"Don't need to be afraid.
No need to be afraid."

The next morning Ros and I are eating a small breakfast when the phone rings. We give each other the eye. Besides Jude, no one has called us on the hotel phone. Remember me mentioning that it was only for emergencies?

"Hello?" I answer, wondering who is on the other line.

"Mel? Hey, it's Maggie! How's the vacation?"

I breathe a sigh, mixed with relief and anticipation. I'm glad no one in my family is dead, but I wonder why Maggie is calling.

"The vacation is good." I send Ros a silent message so she knows it's not an emergency.

Maggie gets straight to the point. "Listen, have you been to that little bookstore in town? They carry all sorts of books that most bookstores don't have—mainly things the celebs who come to the resort drop off or request."

"I walked by it but didn't get to go inside."

"Perfect! As a gift from me, I sent them a case of your book. But I promised that I would send you over to sign it…"

"So all these bored celebrities can read my book on the beach?" I ask her, holding my breath.

"Yes, Mel, and normal people like you and me!"

My heart stops. "But what's the point? No one has heard of me."

"Oh, they just want them to be signed in case you become famous or something. You know. They might even stick you in their stock room with a pen for all I know. But tomorrow at 3:00, okay?"

Before I can answer, I hear the dial tone. Maggie is always straight to the point.

Oh, crap. Not that this is a bad thing, but there's a catch.

I still haven't told Jude.

I was planning on it, but I've been waiting for him to tell me his news before I told him mine. I try to appear happy.

Ros sends me a questioning look.

"Maggie. She wants me to do a book signing."

"And…" She looks confused, trying to figure out why I'm so sad about something that appears like a good thing. But then her eyes light up. "You haven't told Jude about your book, right?"

"No."

"Oh. Well, you better figure something out. When's the signing?"

"Tomorrow."

Crap.

I want to tell him, but I don't know how to break it to him without him getting mad.

Jude comes over for a quick dinner, but we don't get much talking done because Jason shows up, which means that it's time to leave for the bonfire. It's only dusk, but there's supposed to be an open mike time. And, to my surprise, Jude stops at his hotel room to grab his guitar. *Interesting.*

The bonfire is a little past where Jude and I fell asleep the other day. As we are walking by the spot, he sends me a little smile, and my heart jumps.

He feels it too.

We walk side by side, almost brushing up against each other. Almost, but not quite. I'm starting to wish that he would touch me, even a little.

Looking at him, I remember I have something important to tell him.

Wait.

Great. My little voice is back.

We get to the bonfire, and it actually looks professional. There is a concessions stand, and people are listening to radios and watching portable DVD players. It's like a college hangout, minus the alcohol.

The bonfire is rather big. It's nearly sundown, and the little red and orange flames are searching for oxygen. It's pretty romantic.

We all decide on a spot on the sand, but Jude grabs his guitar and goes to a group of people, all obviously musicians, who are excited about being able to share their talent.

Everyone unanimously lets Jude sing, which is weird because there are other guys with guitars there. It's like Jude has been here before and everyone knows who he is.

Jude starts with a prayer, and it's like his voice puts a trance over everyone there. Including me.

I've never heard him play the guitar before, and besides the morning with "Lucy in the Sky with Diamonds," I haven't heard him sing. But, dang, does he have a voice. Rich, smooth as butter, and suitably on key.

Dear Lord, please don't let this vacation be the end of a wonderful relationship.

He starts with a cool song, something about a holiday, and it fits his accent perfectly. My heart is beating a little faster than normal. I look over at Ros and Jason, who are snuggling up several feet away. Something she says makes him laugh, and I can see her blush.

God, I'm so glad that Ros found Jason to carry her through.

Just as I finish my prayer, I look up to see Michael standing only about 10 feet away, intent on Ros and Jason's romantic moment. His eyes are glazed over, almost like he's sad. I'm getting kind of freaked out, because I'm afraid he is going to turn all "tough guy" on us and try to beat Jason up, but to my surprise, Michael almost smiles, then walks away down the beach.

Wow. I have respect for the guy now.

But I decide not to tell Ros about Michael being there. It's going to be my little secret.

Jude is singing a love song now, a mainstream one that's slightly familiar. And he's staring directly at me. His eyes meet mine, and I am sucked away into this dream world where Jude follows me home, we date, and we get married, live in a two-story house, and he sings while I write, and eventually we have two kids and live the American dream. My heart is pounding in my ears, and I can't even hear what he is singing anymore.

All I can see is his eyes, because they are reaching to my soul. Who am I kidding? Jude has taken up a permanent residency in my heart.

I need air.

I glance at Ros and Jason, but they are in their own little world, so I send Jude a little signal that I want something to drink. I walk over to the concessions stand, hugging myself despite the warm wind.

Could it happen?

Is the reason God sent Jude to me because our relationship really is supposed to last forever?

I remember my little voice inside my head, first telling me to wait, then the one that said forever.

Jude and Melody, forever.

I've thought about this before, but somehow it seems a little too good to be true. I don't know his last name. I don't know how old he is. I doubt he would even want to live in America.

I don't really know him at all.

It's been a week, right?

I only imagined that look of love; there's no way he can love me.

Especially not the "forever" kind of love.

Right?

The thought makes me incredibly sad, pained, and alone. I hurry to my destination, feeling cold deep into my bones, even though it's probably 80 degrees out. I can still hear Jude's voice in the distance, but it's fading.

Maybe because it wasn't really there in the first place.

Over by the beverages someone is playing the radio. I step up and order a Mountain Dew as the song switches.

It's a catchy tune.

I pay for my drink and walk a little closer to the radio.

The words are about God, so I'm assuming it's Christian. I've never heard the song, but it sounds really familiar.

The voice sounds familiar.

Rich and smooth as butter.

British.

I can feel my heart stop as I listen to the words. "No," I whisper, stepping farther away.

"And that was Jude Deveraux, formerly of Scars Remain, the most popular Christian band to come out from England. The split from supermodel Alex Corvac has sent Jude into a tailspin. Word has it that he's decided to leave the music industry all together…"

There's more to the broadcast, but I am too busy running down to the ocean to hear.

I'm sick. I collapse onto my knees into the wet sand, the waves splashing onto my legs. Tears are cascading down my face, and my gag reflex has kicked in.

I hope no one is watching. It isn't until after five minutes of dry-heaving that I finally am able to roll over onto my side.

Breathe.

The little voice comes back, this time with something sensible as input. I catch my breath, but the tears don't stop.

Lord, why? Everything was so great!

This was Jude's big secret—he was famous too, but much more than I am. He was in a band, a Christian band. But he didn't tell me.

And the sick part about is that everyone, maybe even Ros, seemed to know about it tonight.

Not to mention a supermodel named Alex thrown into the mix, and I'm just the rebound girl. He's probably been here hundreds of times.

And he's probably met a girl each time.

Yup, Melody Kennedy is probably just another girl that Jude has decided to swoon to his side, making me feel like he's Mr. Right, when really he's only Mr. Right Now!

"Melody?" I hear his voice calling me up on the beach. He probably got worried when it took me 20 minutes to get a soda.

I glance up to see him, and he looks so amazing.

He's searching for me, acting genuinely concerned.

Jerk.

It really does make me sick this time.

I hightail it back to the hotel, not even glancing behind me. I let myself in, probably leaving wet sand all over the hardwood floors.

I don't care.

I bury myself underneath the covers, hoping this is only a dream, and it will all go away.

It doesn't.

Sometime during the night Ros comes in and tries to shake me awake. I pretend to be asleep. After a few minutes she leaves, then whispers to someone outside.

It is probably Jude, checking to make sure that he for sure ruined the life of yet another girl on the island.

I fall back asleep.

Ros comes in again, this time in the morning. She walks over to the blinds and opens my shades.

"Melody Rebekah Kennedy, you better get your butt up and tell me what in the world happened to you last night."

I peek at her through bleary eyes. My head hurts, but my heart hurts more. Unlike all the other pains of love I've ever felt, this is 100 times worse. It feels like a broken heart.

Because I was actually in love with Jude.

I *am* in love with Jude…but does it matter, now that I know he doesn't feel the same?

What makes you think that he doesn't?

I ignore the voice.

Ros stands above me with her hands on her hips. "Mel, Jude was so worried last night. We looked everywhere for you! What in the world made you think it would be okay to run off by yourself?"

"Ros." I shift up on my elbows, trying to get her to listen.

"Furthermore, you scared me. Twice this week, I thought you had been kidnapped and killed."

"Ros."

"Melody, listen to me! What happened to you?"

"He lied to me, Ros. He's famous, but he didn't tell me." I get a word in edgewise.

Finally, she's quiet. And she looks really confused.

"I thought you knew," I whisper.

So I tell her about me not telling Jude who I was and him telling me he had a big decision to make regarding his life, but he wasn't sure what he wanted to do.

And then I tell her about hearing that song on the radio. Jude's song.

By the end of my sappy story, my face is soaked in tears.

But so is hers. A true best friend feels your pain in a time of sorrow.

"Oh, Melody." She crawls into bed with me and gives me a well-needed hug.

I want to fall asleep again, to ignore everything and anything, but I know I can't. Plus, there's this pesky little voice in my head telling me to pray. Like that little voice hasn't done enough damage in my heart to last a lifetime! Oh, well.

God.

I realize I am completely exasperated, and that it's probably not the best way to start off a prayer. I learned long ago that God is like a friend, so we should talk to Him like we would talk to our best friend—comfortably.

So I start over.

God, why? I understand that everything happens in Your timing, and within Your will, but I don't see the point. I've been praying like crazy for Jude and our relationship. I don't see the point of You thrusting us together, making us feel what we are feeling, and then tearing it all away. At first I thought leaving here would tear us apart, but I didn't realize we'd have trials and tribulations—all within two weeks.

I don't understand, but I want to so badly. How could Jude keep something so big from me? I understand that I wasn't being entirely truthful, either, but his secret was so much bigger, so more important than mine. He's been living the life of a star, and I am only beginning to taste it. God, please do something. But I don't know what I want You to do.

Hmmm. *I don't know what I want Him to do.* The thought strikes me as odd.

I think about it for a minute before it hits me: I don't know what I want God to do...*for me.* Do I really deserve to be waited on hand and foot by the Creator? Shouldn't I be thinking about what I should do for God?

And now I'm guilty.

That's the reason!

"Ros, do you think God is punishing me for not letting His will be done?"

She flips over on her side, almost glaring at me. "Do you really think God punishes us for wrong? No. There are consequences of our actions, but that's different. I think God knew this was going to happen, and that He'll find a way to work things out, for better or for worse. That's why it's called faith, Melody."

Faith.

Such a simple, wonderful, five-letter word. I remember thinking that I was so content with my love life, thinking God was working my will in my life. And He was. But it was at that point I decided it didn't matter what I did, because God had wanted Jude and I together, and it happened, so now we could let our feelings run our lives.

I was wrong.

Like Ros said, I was lacking faith.

So I do the thing that I haven't really done since I started this vacation: I pull out my Bible and flip it open to my favorite verse. I found it one day by simply closing my eyes and letting God lead my fingers. I start reading Colossians 2, verse 2, out loud:

"For my concern is that their hearts may be braced (comforted, cheered, and encouraged) as they are knit together in love, that

they may come to have all the abounding wealth and blessings of assured conviction of understanding, and that they may become progressively more intimately acquainted with and may know more definitely and accurately and thoroughly that mystic secret of God, which is Christ the Anointed One."

I close my eyes and let the words flow deep into my soul.

Sorry, I apologize to God. I don't need to tell Him why. He already knows.

I have to face Jude, who is also a mystic secret.

God, I have to leave in five days. I don't want to leave Jude, but I know I must. I hope that there's a future for us, but I understand if there isn't. Although it pains my heart to think of it, I know that I must accept it and be happy with Your plan.

9

"Thought I'd been in love before,
but in my heart I wanted more."

All I want is to go bang on Jude's door and give him a huge hug.

It only took a few hours for me to figure out something: last night I was being extremely selfish and I overreacted.

In fact, he probably is worried sick about me. He probably doesn't even realize that I found out the truth about him.

No matter how much I know that I was wrong, it still doesn't calm my heart from thinking that maybe, possibly, what I thought about Jude was true.

Maybe I am just "one of the girls" in Jude's long history.

But you know what? I have to be content with that, even if it kills me.

And boy, does the thought kill me. I also need to understand that God is letting this happen for a reason.

Lord, I hope I'm wrong.

It's 2:30 in the afternoon, and I have to be somewhere at 3:00.

I take a really quick shower, waking Ros up to come with me. I'm not supposed to go into town alone, remember?

We rush to the store. I tell them who I am, they hand me a pen, and lead me to a table where copies of my book are waiting to be signed.

A young girl is already waiting in line.

I sit down and smile. "I'm Rebekah." I give her my pen name. "Did you want to purchase one of these?"

She gives me a shy, yet familiar smile. A sinking feeling settles into my stomach and is confirmed when she talks.

"I have one of my own, but my brother just bought one more. Can you sign it to Beth Deveraux?" Her perfect British accent stuns me, and I blindly scribble, *To Beth Deveraux. In God's Love, Rebekah Kennedy.*

Just peachy.

"I can't believe you're making me buy one of these." A tall, handsome man comes to a shocked stop in front of the table.

"Jude," I whisper.

I panic and search for the comfort of my best friend.

Rosalyn has vanished into a corner, far, far away.

He looks down at the book on the table. "Rebekah Kennedy?" he asks, stepping forward. It's my pen name, which is really my name minus my first name. I didn't like the idea of people knowing who I am just by hearing my name, assuming I ever become that popular. *Shut up, Mel.*

Nevertheless, he's talking to me.

"Jude Deveraux," I say quietly, noticing that his eyes flicker with surprise.

He didn't know that I knew, but then I didn't know that he knew.

Wow, I am confusing myself.

Jude looks me straight in the eyes. "It shouldn't surprise me. I guessed that the reason you fled last night was because someone told you. "

I shake my head, averting my gaze to my feet. Pretty feet, they are. Cute toes.

"Your voice was on the radio," I manage.

I start signing the books, knowing that they are the only things standing between me and the door.

"You could have just told me, you know. Simple as that."

I glance up. "It's complicated."

"Melody, it's only what you make it."

"How old are you?" I blurt out.

He looks confused by my question. "Twenty-four."

I nod. "Only 24, and already a rock star. Must have been a lot of work." My tone is slightly sarcastic, and I can tell it hurts him a little.

He sighs, then comes and sits on the table that holds my books. "I want you to understand that I am still the same person you met, Miss Melody. Nothing's changed." He shrugs. "It's easier for people to like me, the real me, without them knowing that I'm slightly rich and famous. It's also easier for me to relax without worrying about all that...stuff. That's why I came on holiday. I needed to forget everything and make up my blasted mind about what I'm going to do with my life."

Even with my breakthrough talk with God this afternoon, the pain is surfacing to my heart again. Tears blur my vision and cloud my mind.

"But what about Alex Corvac?" Pain shoots in his eyes, and I look away. "I can't talk right now, Jude. Meet me at the beach, our place, later, okay?"

He nods and then walks out the door, followed by a confused Beth.

I turn to the sales clerk, who has apparently been watching our conversation with great amusement.

"Did he pay for this?" I gesture toward Jude's forgotten copy of my book.

She nods. "Can I take it to him?" She nods again.

Ros suddenly reappears. I can tell from the look in her eye that she might appear nonchalant, but she heard every word that took place. I quickly sign the rest of the books, making my hand hurt in a small period of time.

Ros walks me partially back to the hotel but stops when we hit the beach. She swivels toward me, hope in her eyes. "Melody, I know that sometimes we can get carried away, but I honestly think that God has a big plan for you and Jude. Don't mess things up."

Then she walks away. At first I'm slightly hurt by her comment, but I know she didn't mean anything by it. Her job as my best friend is not only to share my pain, but to kick me in the butt when I'm being stupid.

And stupid I have been.

I run, faster than I have before (third time's a charm!) through the sand to get to the spot on the beach that I refer to as "ours."

Jude's not there. I hate to admit it, but my heart breaks a little more. I don't know what to do, so I sit on the sand.

But seconds go by, and then he's next to me.

He's the strong, silent type, I realize, and that's exactly what I need to keep me in line.

"It's like we have to start all over," I whisper to the ocean.

"I must be frank with you, Miss Melody. And keep in mind that no matter how we appear, no man is really good with words. I don't want to mess things up." He pauses for a long time. "You're different."

I chuckle sarcastically. "Great, I'm different. My first thought, when I found out who you were, was that I was just another girl you met on the beach on one of your vacations. Not to mention the supermodel."

He shakes his head vigorously. "No, not at all. I actually...wow, this is embarrassing...but I've never had a girlfriend. I don't really know...what to do."

"But what about...?"

"Alex and I were friends, and that's it. You have no idea how much the press can mesh things. We were seen together once, and then suddenly, we're engaged. She's really in love with one of my former band mates."

I can tell that it's the truth, and he's not just making excuses.

My tall, dark, and handsome Jude is a dating virgin. It's one step up from being a plane virgin, mind you.

"I've kind of gone out before, but nothing with substance." I pitch my ridiculousness into the conversation.

"Same here. I mean, I went to dances and such, but nothing that lasted to a second date." He takes a deep breath. "What I mean is, I don't know how to go about a relationship." He looks extremely uncomfortable, and it's cute because he is more uncomfortable with it than I would be in his situation.

It's adorable; I promise.

"And...I want to start a relationship with you, Melody." This time, he stares right into my eyes.

I was totally not expecting him to say that. I choke on...well, I assume my saliva, because it's the only thing in my throat. I was expecting him to apologize, to suggest we start over (like I had), but not to ask me out.

"But what about my book? You know, the one that poisons the minds of young girls? We both kept things from each other."

"Everything's in the open now, and we're both stronger for it."

I breathe deeply, trying to process everything that's happened.

Wait. He said he wanted to start a relationship with me. But he did not specify what kind of relationship.

I think slowly, trying to figure out what to do.

Thump. A thought hits me. *Duh.*

"Jude, will you pray for us?"

He appears pleased at my suggestion, then clasps his hands in front of him. "Father God, we both want Your will in our lives and in our relationship, but we need Your guidance. Lord, please bless us and keep us. May Your grace shine upon us. And may our hearts be knit together in Your love. Amen."

"May our hearts be knit together in Your love," I repeat. Sound familiar?

"Yeah, it's from this verse in Colossians that I read this afternoon. It's an amazing passage."

I'm sure I looked shocked. "Jude, that's my favorite verse. Colossians 2, verse 2, right?"

He grins and then sends a silent glance upward. "I was praying about you this afternoon, and I felt a need to go to Colossians. Incredible, isn't it? How subtly God works? I was so uneasy about my life, and the decisions I have to make, and how I treated you poorly. I should have just told you."

I nod.

Turns out that, even though Jude has flaws, he relies on God to see him through. I understand completely what he means.

I also realize that we do have to start over, in a sense, but it will be a better start. So I do the obvious.

I stick out my hand. "My name is Melody Rebekah Kennedy, I am 19 years old, and I just published my first novel."

Jude looks horrified. Not exactly the effect I was trying to achieve.

"Your novel! I left it at the bookstore."

"Don't worry; I have it." I pat my tote bag. "But you don't get it back until I figure out what to write in it. You wanted it signed, right?"

He laughs, and once again I realize how wonderful his laugh is. And how God can heal all wounds, and how trivial our small fight was. But at the same time, it was essential for this step to be taken.

"Okay, my name is Jude Michael Deveraux. I'm 24. When I was 17, a few buddies and I started a Christian band called Scars Remain. It hit the charts before I was 20, but we broke up that year. Ever since then I have been doing solo music in Europe."

"It's nice to meet you, Jude."

He holds his hand out to mine, and I'm shocked by the electricity that runs through my fingers, down my spine, and out my toes.

"*It's electrifyin'!*" (*Greased lightning, go greased lightning…*)

Okay, I realize that I'm weird, but look past that for a moment.

Let's recap: Jude just touched me for the first time since I met him.

Wow, am I glad I waited.

And what's really cool about this is that I felt fireworks, and judging by his expression, Jude did too. Oh, happy day!

I must…calm….down….

Change the subject!

But Jude is still holding my hand….

I clear my throat. "So, your big decision. Tell me about it."

Jude's mood changes swiftly. "I'm so sick of it, Melody. I never went to university; I never had the chance to grow up. Yes, I love my music, and I love glorifying God through it, but I want a chance to just be me without having a name stuck to it. I don't want to be 'Jude Deveraux, singer/songwriter extraordinaire.' I just want to be Jude."

"I understand how being in the limelight changes things, but why can't you be yourself?"

"I'm probably a little more popular in Europe than I let on. I want to go to university, but I can't go anywhere over there for fear I'll get bombarded within a week."

"So your decision was to leave the music industry and go to college?"

"Lame as it sounds, yes."

"I've been trying to get out of going to college to write."

He shoots me an admiring gaze. "And you're going to be amazing. You've attended some schooling, haven't you?"

I nod. "One year of community college. Despite wanting to be completely done and adult, I've applied to go to a Christian college starting in March."

Is this news to you? I sent in the application around the time that I heard my book was going to be published, but I just decided in the last ten minutes to actually go. I feel pretty confident, and somehow I think that this is what God has been leading me up to.

"Tell me about this college."

I pause and then start to get excited. I can hardly believe it myself. "It's right in my hometown but was just started last year. It focuses on the arts—especially music and writing, my two favorite things. It gives a Christian approach to glorifying God with your spiritual gifts."

"Sounds like the perfect university for you."

"My parents seem to like it because it means I wouldn't be moving too far away from home."

"Do you get along with them, your parents?"

"More so than when I was a kid." I sigh. "I really miss them right now."

I look over the water, where the sun is falling. It reminds me of sleeping soundly next to Jude. Too bad I don't remember it much.

"It's getting late." I state the obvious. "This has been an emotionally exhausting day for me."

"And for me as well." He digs our hands into the sand, and I feel the warmth of it.

"Jude?"

"Yes, Miss Melody?"

"You're right. You're still the same person. It's possible, though, that I respect you more now than I did before. I understand what you've been going through. I don't even want people to know my real name."

Jude stands, letting go of my hand for a split second before offering it to help me up. The second touch of the day, but no less exhilarating.

"I know we've talked about this before, but do you wonder why

God has let this all happen?"

I am forward with my analysis. "I was praying about that this afternoon, and I can only think that He has an incredible plan for our future. Neither Ros nor I believe that this will be the end of my relationship with you."

He looks flattered. "So you talk about me to Ros, eh?"

"Of course. What else do girls do than talk about the men in their lives?"

"Good point."

We walk back to the hotel in comfortable silence, hand in hand, while the sun sets.

God's creation really is beautiful, isn't it?

And I'm not looking at the sun.

Ros isn't there when I get home, so I go to my room and fall asleep.

She wakes me first thing in the morning. It's, like, really early.

Okay, so it's 8 a.m.

Now, I'm not always happy when someone takes away my beauty sleep, but this time I'm content.

"So?" She stands over me, looking for answers.

I break into a grin.

"Do you know that Paul McCartney song?" I ask groggily as I stretch my arms into the sky.

She looks at me like I'm crazy.

I really need to get this poor girl into oldies, and fast.

"*Maybe I'm amazed by the way you love me all the time...maybe I'm amazed by the way I really need you...,*" I drone, thinking that Jude would be disappointed in my singing voice.

But, hey, it's early, so it's not getting much better than this.

Ros arches her eyebrows, giving me a look I've grown used to. "It went that well, huh?"

We call in room service for breakfast, and I relate the whole story, bit by bit, without leaving one minute detail out, while eating sausage gravy and biscuits.

Have I mentioned how much I love sausage gravy and biscuits? It's a talent few skilled gossipers possess—the ability to chew food without making the other person see it and wanting to puke.

Today I discovered that I have that talent.

"I'm excited for you," Ros adds.

It's my turn to raise my eyebrows. "You don't seem very excited."

"I'm getting the blues, Mel. Counting today, that only leaves four days until we hop on a jet plane."

I giggle. Okay, so maybe she knows the music a little bit. But I think it's "leaving on a jet plane," right?

"Then today is you-and-me day, no guys, in which we will go lay on the beach, read books, and tan."

"Agreed." She laughs wholeheartedly.

It's only 10 a.m., but it's already at least 80 degrees outside. I pull on a white suit, one of my more modest tankinis, and lather suntan lotion onto my skin. No use in burning myself again like last time. I secretly call Jude and end up leaving a message on his room phone, telling him my plans for the day.

It feels good, knowing that Jude will probably listen to my message and smile.

As a last thought, I grab Jude's copy of my book and a ballpoint pen, in case I think of something clever to write. After all, it may be the only thing he has to remember me by, but somehow I doubt it.

This time we're able to grab a spot close to the water that is right in front of the hotel; usually the space is taken up, but I assume it's because a lot of people left over the weekend. It seems emptier.

Within seconds, Ros is completely engrossed in some vampire novel (again, don't ask). I close my eyes and let my imagination run wild. This is exactly what I had imagined the whole vacation being like—Ros and I conked out on the beach, day-in and day-out, tanning and reading through the stack of novels that we brought. So far, the only thing I've completed is my John Lennon biography, and it was a mass market edition, only about 100 pages long.

I'm lost in thought, and the only thing I can think of is the lyrics of a worship song by Michael W. Smith, "The Heart of Worship":

When the music fades, and all is stripped away
And I simply come.
Longing just to bring, something that's of worth,
That will bless Your heart.
I'll bring You more than a song, for a song in itself
Is not what You have required.
You search much deeper within, through the ways things appear,
You're looking into my heart…
I'm coming back to the heart of worship,
And it's all about You…it's all about You, Jesus.
I'm sorry, Lord, for the things I've made it,
Because it's all about You, it's all about You, Jesus.

The song reminds me of Jude, and I think of how great of a struggle it must have been for him to leave his music behind. Honestly, I think that wherever he goes, he'll end up in a music ministry, but that's a choice he'll have to make.

Furthermore, the song also reminds me that in whatever we do, everything is really all about Jesus: my writing, Jude's music, Rosalyn's…whatever she does.

Putting Jude Deveraux aside, I have matured this trip. Ros thought so days ago, and I think the realization has finally hit me harder. Before, when I found out Jude was famous, it would have taken days, maybe weeks, for me to push myself to forgive him, and then finally realize that it wasn't really his fault in the first place. This time, it took me a matter of about 15 hours.

I've also matured spiritually. I've always been in love with Jesus, but I don't ever think you stop learning and improving yourself, trying to achieve the goal of becoming alike Him.

Finally, my heart has matured, mostly because it's fallen in love.

Yes, I finally admit it. I've fallen in love.

Now, don't get all excited and jump up and down.

I don't know if it's really possible to fall in love with someone in a week and a half, but I can be honest and tell you that, even though I've never tasted love before, I am pretty sure that this is it. It's based on more of a mutual respect and friendship than it is on simply…feelings.

And it's based on God.

I start humming the tune to "Maybe I'm Amazed" again, and I realize that it's the perfect thing to write in Jude's book. I take it out of my tote and look at the cover. It's a cute design, with a girl's face reflected in all these different shiny surfaces, but only bits and pieces, never her whole outline. I had it made perfectly, because the girl in the story feels pulled in so many different directions, never feeling whole. Let's just say it's slightly autobiographical in that sense.

I open the front page and write in my best penmanship: *To Jude—Maybe I'm Amazed.*

The pen hovers over the next words. Do I say *from? Love? Sincerely?*

Forever.

Oh, that little voice tends to be right, doesn't it?

Forever, Melody Rebekah Kennedy.

I shut the book and place it safely in my tote bag.

I close my eyes and fall asleep under the warm afternoon sun.

Ros rouses (tongue twister!) me about an hour later, claiming that she's absolutely hungry and has never been hungrier in her life (and I think she says that every single day, too).

Either way, we hop, skip, and jump the 100 feet back to our room. I indeed notice that I left sandy footprints the other night, and Ros, being the neat freak she is (sarcasm) hasn't cleaned them up yet. So while she's off getting yummy food for us, I sweep, put away neglected dishes, and straighten throw pillows.

Then, as I'm standing there thinking what else to do, something hits me. Both Ros and I encouraged our families to email us, but I don't think either of us has even gotten out the computer.

It takes me a minute to find my laptop because it's buried underneath nine days of dirty clothes. I let it boot up, then type in the hotel's wireless internet password to connect me to Hotmail. I have about 20 messages, most of which are spam. I read the ones from people I know:

Mom: Mel, you are probably really busy, but I wanted to let you know we love you and miss you!

Maggie: SENDING CASE OF BOOKS TO LOCAL STORE FOR SIGNING. CALL WITH DETAILS.

Craig (Little brother): Hey smelly Melly. Mom says I should write you to say hi, but I really want you to get back into town. Without you here, I am the only person the parentals can pick on. Come quick…save me!

Allie (Second best friend who got left home): Mel! How are you? Oh, I bet you are so tan! You have to let me know what's happening!

I reply first to Mom, simply telling her that I am fine, alive, and that I miss them too. Maggie wouldn't read my email if I replied and she needs to know that writing in *Caps Lock* is NOT okay, and Craig is just stupid sometimes. Allie, however, deserves a bit more merit.

Allie, it's amazing, I'm a little more red than brown, but I have met someone…will tell you everything when I get home! Ros says hi.

Ros really does say hi, because she's arrived back already with food and is looking over my shoulder to see what I am writing.

"Next time, we'll bring her," Ros says with complete confidence.

I turn. "What makes you think there'll be a next time?"

Ros smiles. "This is your inspiring trip, remember? You're supposed to be able to whip out another novel within two years or you're void of contract."

She reminds me of the reason I am here, not to meet amazing guys and get a really great tan, but so I can relax in the midst of the chaos that has become my life.

I have no doubt that I can write another book within my two-year deadline, and I think it will probably be even better than my last one.

Ros and I eat, then head to the town's gift shop to get trinkets for the "kids" back home. I find an adorable purple butterfly pendant that I can give to Allie for being such a good sport.

"Mel!" Ros apparently found something wonderful, because she starts yelling my name across the room. I smile apologetically to the clerk, who is staring wide-eyed at Ros's behavior.

"Rosalyn," I hiss like a mother, "behave yourself in public!"

"Look." She points to a little pocket stone shaped into a heart.

But the words written on it shock me: It's the Colossians 2 verse. When I worked at a Christian bookstore, I never once saw that verse on a gift item. What are the odds?

I enthusiastically hug Ros, then grab the stone. It's the perfect farewell gift for Jude.

10

*"Seems like all I really was doing
was waiting for you."*

Three days and counting.

Oh, the horror!

But the neat thing is that there is a formal dance tonight (the one I discovered early in our vacation), and Jude and Jason have invited both Rosalyn and me, including a dinner beforehand.

It's only morning, but Ros and I are doing what any girl our age does before a huge event: beautifying.

I'm sure that if either of our dates were to walk in right now, they would bolt screaming from the room.

Green facial mask is spread on our faces, our hair is greasy with leave-in moisturizer, our lips are slightly pale with lip exfoliate, our toes are freshly polished and in pink little toe holder-thingies, our legs are covered with hair removal cream, and we are walking around in our underwear.

We look like monsters.

The cool thing is that we are watching chick flicks, and this time we are *both* eating carrots. We are having a blast!

The not-cool thing is that we can't sit on anything (for fear of staining the furniture with Nair) or smile (because the face masks are drying and we don't want them to crack).

It's actually pretty funny, because we are watching *You've Got Mail* and it's hard not to laugh, or cry, during this movie.

I know I have wet streaks running down my face when Tom Hanks and Meg Ryan are kissing in the park at the end of the movie. *"I wanted it to be you."*

We both disappear into our bathrooms to shower and de-mask.

The dance is at six, so dinner is at four, and it's now two, so Ros and I do each other's hair up in cute little up-dos with ringlets falling over our faces (mine natural, hers created) and apply only a sheer layer of makeup to our well-tanned faces. We both put on our two most fancy dresses that we each only brought one of (and that we had to take advantage of the hotel's drycleaners for). Both dresses have tulle straps and waistbands, and are floor length. Ros's dress is black, and mine is white.

Classic.

Underneath, we both wear flip-flops because neither of us can walk straight in heels.

No one's going to see our feet anyway.

At promptly 3:45, there's a knock on the door. This time, both Jude and Jason are at the front, holding red rose corsages to put on our wrists.

Romantics.

I'm sure, if we were leaving the hotel, that they would have had a limo waiting. However, they nicely walk us to the elevator, treating us like princesses.

Jason is touching Rosalyn's arm, ever so slightly, and I'm sure it's sending a tingling sensation up her spine.

Although Jude looks comfortable, like maybe he's getting used to this almost-dating thing, he isn't touching me. I must admit that I'm happy Jude and I don't have that kind of relationship—I can be sure there's no way this feeling I have is based on physical touch. But at the same time, I hope and wish with all my might that I could just get one…little…kiss.

A real kiss. I've had tiny, meaningless kisses before, but nothing with one hint of the emotion and love that I have for Jude.

Love.

Yes, I know I love him. I said that before, but I have no plan in revealing my feelings for him until I am led—namely, if he says it first. And although I have a slight notion (maybe just a little one…) that he might feel the same, tonight is not the right time to say it.

I don't know when it will be the right time, but you know what?

I don't need to.

I have faith.

At least I can say that for the first time this week.

Both men get out of the elevator first and stand on either side. It's like they are trying to open the door for us, but they can't because the doors don't open that way. It's sweet, nonetheless.

We arrive upstairs at the restaurant, which is completely packed. I'm assuming everyone had the same idea we did. I am about to panic, wondering if either male forgot the importance of a reservation, but Jude steps up to the hostess.

"Deveraux, party of four."

The pretty blond flashes a flirtatious smile at my love, and I fume. Jude, bless his heart, doesn't even seem to notice. He is too busy staring at me.

Jason and Jude offer us the inside seats and then scoot in next to us. Jude's thigh is touching mine, and I can hardly concentrate on anything else. There's a mild, comfortable chatter around the table as we wait for the waitress.

Jude orders for me, something that sounds like mashed potatoes and chicken gravy. Mmmmm.

Jason orders a rare steak, split for two.

Gross. Both Ros and I hate our steaks rare.

I send her a look that says, "I'll slip you something of mine to eat." Ros smiles back gratefully. See how awesome we are?

"So, I leave tomorrow night." Jason interrupts everyone's thoughts. Ros looks sad, but I can tell she was expecting this. I make a note to tell her tonight that she can be with Jason all day tomorrow, up until the second he leaves.

Jude nods. "I leave Friday morning."

I fake a smile. "We leave that same afternoon."

Although we are all happy right now, it's also obvious that we're all sad to be leaving vacation and to be leaving each other. I will even miss Jason, and I've barely spoken five words to him since I've met him. I'm just glad Ros ended up with him and not Michael.

And no, I still haven't mentioned that time on the beach. I don't think I will.

Our food comes, so we laugh over a few things while we eat. I think of something I hadn't told Ros.

"Do you remember," I set down my fork, "the morning you let Jude in to wait for me?"

She nods. "Yes."

"Well, you could have warned me. I walked out wearing my oversized Beatles T-shirt...and nothing else!" This causes laughter to bubble from Ros and Jason, and for Jude to look slightly embarrassed. I touch his knee and give it a squeeze. I want him to know that I am here for him.

He smiles back, that melting smile that I'm sure caused every woman in the restaurant to sigh.

Sometimes I forget how good-looking he is on the outside. Happily, I've fallen in love with his insides first.

We finish our dinners with me insisting that Ros have the rest of my chicken because I simply cannot eat it, but I don't want it to go to waste. Luckily for her, Jason ate most of the steak himself without realizing that Ros hadn't touched it.

Declining on dessert, the four of us walk the few feet from the restaurant to the ballroom. Now, all I know about this dance is that it's formal. I don't know if there's an itinerary, but it looks like there's going to be a live band.

Jude and I dance, swaying to the music of a quartet of gentlemen, but I can tell that something's making him nervous. After about the fifth song, I'm thinking the worst, that maybe he's breaking up with me before we are even dating, but the music stops and someone comes to the microphone. And we haven't gotten to slow-dance yet.

"Now we have some special music from Jude Deveraux!"

I stare, rather confused, at my wonderful Jude. He squeezes my hand, then heads up to the stage and grabs a guitar that I recognize as his own, now that I pay attention.

Ros finds me. "What is he doing?"

"I…don't….know," I stutter.

Jason looks like he may have an idea, but he's keeping it a secret.

Men.

Jude grabs the mike, quite naturally, and starts talking. I can tell that people are amazed by his thick British accent, and I am as well. I almost forget it sometimes.

"This is an older song, but I've met someone this week that brings all the feelings of this song to surface." He's staring right at me, and a few people notice, turning to look at me as well. It's kind of embarrassing, but I can't help but grin.

Jude's going to sing me a song.

"This is for Miss Melody."

The band is now playing back-up, and I'm slightly freaked out by the song they start.

Jude's voice, clear as day, starts singing just like Paul McCartney. "Maybe I'm amazed at the way you love me all the time, maybe I'm afraid of the way I love you. Maybe I'm amazed at the way you pulled me out of time, and hung me on a line. Maybe I'm amazed at the way I really need you."

Ros grabs my arm and stares at me with this shocked expression. "Isn't this the song…?" she asks, knowing for a fact that yes, it is the song I was singing yesterday, as well as what I wrote in Jude's book.

And he didn't know about it.

"I'm a man, maybe I'm a lonely man, who's in the middle of something, that he doesn't really understand. Babe, I'm a man, and maybe you're the only woman who could ever help me, Baby won't you help me understand," he sings loudly. I can't tell, but it almost looks like there are tears on his face.

No way. It's probably just sweat.

"Maybe I'm amazed at the way you're with me all the time, maybe I'm afraid of the way I leave you. Maybe I'm amazed at the way you help me sing my song," he glances at me, "right me when I'm wrong…maybe I'm amazed at the way I really need you."

I realize that couples, including Jason and Ros, are dancing all around me. Here I am, standing foolishly in the middle of the floor, staring up at Jude.

"I'm amazed…by you." He finishes to applause. People have stopped dancing, and a lot of the women are staring enviously at me.

(Insert evil laugh!)

Jude walks down the stairs, and people move to make way for him. He comes directly to me. We stand there, staring at each other, neither of us talking or moving.

I'm in a trance. My heart is beating so fast that it's going to pop right out of my chest.

It's been several moments, and the band has started playing again.

Jude's staring at me with his amazingly green eyes, and I'm lost in them.

I'm lost in him.

Forever.

Finally, he reaches over and grabs me by the waist, pulling me close to him. His touch about paralyzes me, because I have never been this close to him, and it's driving me crazy.

We sway to the music. It's a slow number, probably original, but I wouldn't notice if they were up there doing the Macarena.

I can tell we're both completely shocked and in awe at what we see in each other's faces. And now I'm thinking about one of the lines in the song, "Maybe I'm afraid by the way I love you," and it makes me wonder.

He wouldn't have sung that song unless it was true.

Right?

Wait.

My little voice is back, and it stops me from uttering the three little words that I can never take back.

And even if I had said them, I wouldn't want to take them back.

Because they are so true, especially at this moment.

Jude smiles, and I remember how much I thought he looked like Colin Farrell.

Nah. He looks like Jude.

But I smile back, wondering if he thinks I look like anyone. A little bigger, crazy, curly hair, and blue eyes?

I think I'm pretty much an individual.

I nestle my head onto his shoulder, and he tightens his grip on my waistline. We're lost in our own little world.

It's majestic.

I never want this night to end.

Two hours later, it does.

Jason had to get back to his room to pack, but Jude walked Ros and I back to our room, obviously because he is right next door.

He looks at Ros. "I would like to see if it's alright with you that

I kidnap Melody for the day tomorrow." Then he shifts his gaze to me, penetrating my eyes. "I have something special planned."

Ros good-naturedly holds up her hands. "You can have her. I don't want her!"

I push her into the wall.

Jude smiles. "Good night, Rosalyn. Miss Melody."

We walk into our room and wait a minute until we hear Jude's door shut securely.

Then we both explode into a fit of giggles.

11

"Don't need to be alone.
No need to be alone."

When Jude had mentioned a surprise, I didn't think it included being awakened at 5 a.m., but apparently I was wrong.

Completely, dead wrong.

So, there's this knock on my bedroom door at 4:54, and I naturally assume it is Rosalyn, but it's not.

It's Jude, standing there looking cheerful. He manages to get me out of bed, which is a great feat. I'm glad I wore pajama pants last night instead of only my underwear.

I'm sure Jude is glad, too.

The weird thing is that there is an outfit set out for me on my bedroom chair. This, plus the fact Jude managed to get into our hotel room, makes me think Ros was in on it. She could have at least set the alarm.

I am almost upset, but all of my potential anger is wiped away when Jude and I get outside and I see the sunrise. It's perfect, without any clouds, just with hundreds of shades of purple and pink, mixed together in one big artistic setting.

You're amazing, God. Your creation is magnificent, and I can't believe that I get to live in it every day of my life.

Jude slips to his patio and brings me back a steaming cup of Jamaican coffee.

Yup, I'm in love with him!

We start walking down the beach in the direction of the pier, and suddenly I know where we're going.

Waterfalls!

My mood takes a visible pick-me-up, and Jude and I walk in complete silence in the sand.

We reach the pier in about ten minutes and walk some more.

And more.

And more.

"Jude?"

He turns to me, surprised. The boy had been lost in thought.

"How much farther?"

He smiles. "Getting a little tired, are you? Don't worry; it's only about five minutes away!"

Jude zones out again, but true to his word, about five minutes later we come to a path. "Okay, Miss Melody, we need to go up and we'll be there."

My jaw drops. Up?

I knew it! He thinks I'm fat and is creating exercise in order for me to get into shape. There is no other reasonable explanation.

Lucky for me, Jude seems to have snapped out of his train of thought and has now decided to pay me the attention that I so crave.

"So, Miss Melody, are you planning on publishing another book?" he asks, keeping a good three-foot distance ahead of me.

I'm panting already.

"I have a contract that states that I have to have a second book within two years. I'm sure I will, because I already have a few ideas in mind. It's finding the time to actually sit down and write without interruptions that really makes it hard. That's why I took a leave of absence from my job."

"At the bookstore, right?"

I nod. "I love it. I might want to open my own someday. I want it to be a lot like this bookstore in town; I want to have unique and local things that chain bookstores don't have. That way I can be different and won't really have to compete with the large businesses."

"That's a great idea." He looks thoughtful. "I've always wanted to open a music store. I was so frustrated at the local ones in Liverpool. They never had what you wanted or needed, and their employees didn't know a thing."

I chuckle. "Sounds like we are a couple of everyday entrepreneurs."

Until now, the path had been easy and relatively flat. Unfortunately, as I look ahead, it's going to get a bit rougher.

Jude seems to sense my despair and turns around. "Want to catch a breather before the hard stuff starts?"

We stop. "How on earth can you climb this without panting?"

"I did it yesterday, when you and Rosalyn were busy getting ready for the dance."

I roll my eyes at him. Figures.

After a minute, we start up again. It's a fairly steep incline, and more than once Jude stops and offers his hand to help me up a step.

Each time, I gasp at how real his touch feels and the spot is left tingling. *I'm never going to wash my hands,* I think childishly.

The path widens and flattens out a bit, and I am left feeling disappointed. Now there isn't an excuse for Jude to touch me.

A couple of minutes later, I start to hear the crashing of water. I think we're almost there, but it's up another hill. This time we actually have to climb it.

"Almost there, Hun."

I stop. Jude just called me "Hun"! My first pet name!

Unfortunately, the shock knocks me off balance. I lose my footing on the hill and start to slide back down the dirt.

"Jude!"

In a flash, he is right above me, his strong hands grabbing mine and lifting me to safety. I'm almost crying, knowing that it would be pretty far down.

To my surprise, Jude envelops me in a hug, and I can feel the sticky sweat on the back of his T-shirt. It's incredibly sexy and definitely worth the despair of almost falling to my pitiful death.

Okay, so it really wasn't that far down.

"Melody, are you okay?"

I nod, wanting to act like a child so Jude can stop and kiss all my boo-boos. But I am more grown up than that, so we start hiking again. This time, though, Jude makes sure I am climbing in front of him so he can catch me if I fall. I want to remind him that I am probably about the same weight as him, but I figure he can lift that much in weights, or more.

Have I mention how defined his arms are? Or how completely blinded I am by my love that every little thing (including the fresh smell coming off him) is perfect?

We reach a clearing at the bottom of the waterfall. I take a moment to discreetly sniff my armpit to make sure that I don't smell as fresh as he does.

I could use some body spray, but I think I'll make it.

"Melody." Jude is standing on a cement platform with a bench. It's weird that they were able to haul all that concrete up that path....

Then I walk up to Jude and take a quick look at my right.

There are cement stairs.

About three dozen of them, slowly, graciously, nicely curving down to the first path we were on. Right next to it is a dirt road.

I do the only logical thing a girl in my position would.

I smack him. Hard.

"Ouch!" Jude whines, but his accent totally makes it hotter than it should be.

"Jude," I smile sweetly, "why couldn't we have taken the stairs?"

He grins. "I thought the hike would be more fun."

I raise my eyebrows. *Men!*

He shrugs. "Don't worry; we'll take them down. Meanwhile," he steers me into the woods about 20 feet, "there's something that you have to see."

Jude leads me into paradise. There's a fresh pond sitting coolly at the bottom of a large, cascading waterfall. Moss is growing up the sides, and it makes the rocks underneath the water look green. It is surrounded by trees, and the only thing you can hear is water and chirping from birds.

"It's amazing."

"It surely is."

I turn, and Jude isn't looking at the waterfall.

For a few seconds, he stares deeply into my eyes, and I am memorized by his very own pools of green. However, his gaze shifts off to the side, where I now notice is a small building with bathrooms and lockers inside (or at least the sign posted says that there are).

He disappears into it for a second and then comes out carrying a basket and a backpack.

It's hilarious, because he looks like Mary Poppins. The first thing to come out of his bag is a blanket, then his swimming trunks, then two inflatable water mattresses, then bug repellant, then sunscreen, then two flashlights…I can't begin to figure out how he got that all in there!

But he goes to work setting up a little picnic area on the grass. After several minutes, he looks at me and gestures to the blanket.

I'm flattered because he actually took the time to plan this out, and so far, besides the hike (which I admit was fun), everything has been perfect.

I gladly pull up a spot on the blanket right next to him. We just lay there in silence, listening to the sounds of nature around us. Then I can feel him roll over to face me. I do the same, so now we are staring into each other's eyes.

"Melody," he says carefully, "we are both leaving tomorrow."

"I know," I whisper, sadness creeping into my voice. I was hoping that he wouldn't mention it. I get too depressed when I think about leaving him.

"Don't be sad, Miss Melody. I am certain God has great plans for you."

He said "you"…not "us."

I try not to reveal my disappointment. I can tell he's not done talking yet.

Jude takes a deep breath. "I still haven't fully decided what I'm going to do. Part of me wants to kidnap you and keep you here forever, but the other part knows that it is time for both of us to leave and to face our lives and responsibilities."

Okay, by now my heart's racing, and I wish he would just get to the point! But he looks really, really uncomfortable. Shy. Scared.

"What I mean is…" He fishes into his backpack. "I wrote you a song. I don't have my guitar, but you can imagine it with music."

He hands me the lyrics and he sings with his eyes closed. From memory.

This is my song:

You're the sound, you're the tune,
and you're enough to make me swoon,
Oh, Melody.
It's the way you make me feel;
I'm so scared that it's not real,
Oh, Melody.

I'm so crazy inside;

I don't know what's right.
All I can know
Is how you make me feel;
Oh, Melody.

It's about time
That you entered my life.
I've been waiting for you
For so long now—
Oh, Melody.

I've been stuck inside my warp drive.
I've been shoved around,
And I've been knocked down.
But the day I met you
I came unglued...

And all I can say
Is I want you to stay;
Please don't go away...
Oh, Melody.

Obviously, by the time Jude finishes the last note, I'm bawling. He sings my name like this: "Mellow-di." It's cute. Really cute.

It makes me glad that I didn't have time to put on makeup this morning; otherwise I would have smeared mascara running down my face.

I smile. "It's beautiful."

He leans toward me. "You're beautiful, Miss Melody—more so than words can even begin to describe, but I did my best."

Jude is about an inch from my face' and looking into my eyes for a clue. He's going to kiss me.

And this time, there is no little voice telling me to wait.

So I let my lips part ever so slightly, and I close my eyes.

113

In seconds, Jude's warm lips are against mine, and my heart is probably beating so loud that Ros could hear it back at the hotel room.

Hallelujah!

Then it's over.

I open my eyes, only to see Jude staring at me.

And he's happy.

"You have no idea how much I've wanted to do that since you ran into me in the hall and knocked all my towels over."

I laugh. "I thought you would have forgotten all about that already!"

He gets serious. "I won't ever forget a single thing about you. No matter what happens, I will remember this day always, Melody, whether I ever see you again or not. I wanted to make it perfect."

"It is perfect."

There are about 20 Beatles' songs running through my head all at the same time. Love songs.

Jude and I spend the day lying out on the blanket. We try to go swimming, but the waterfall is too cold, so we decide to head back down to the beach. There we meet with Ros and Jason to bid him farewell; then the three of us have a late dinner.

It was the perfect day.

12

"It's real love."

“ I *t's the end of the world as we know it...*”
The song is the first thing that pops into my head the
next morning.

It's our last day here, but Ros and I will spend two days in Dallas until our flight to Seattle.

But Jude won't be in Dallas. Jude is flying back to England in two hours.

I take special time getting ready this morning—my hair is actually frizz-free, and I am wearing a full face of makeup for only the second or third time in the last two weeks.

Ros and I don't leave the hotel until three, so I have plenty of time to pack after I see Jude off.

I have wrapped, in plain brown paper, Jude's copy of my book and the heart with the Colossians verse on it, and a small piece of paper with my contact information.

They are sitting on my nightstand, waiting.

At 10:52, I force myself to walk out the door. Jude and I agreed to meet at our spot on the beach. From there he would walk up to the town (a short distance) to meet his family.

I feel like I am walking to my own funeral. I actually have to push every muscle in my body to keep going. This is a horrible, horrible day.

It only takes a couple minutes to get there, but Jude is already waiting, a package in his hand. His curly hair is blowing in the wind. He's wearing faded blue jeans and a black dress shirt.

He looks every bit the rock star that he is.

I walk straight into his waiting arms.

"Melody," he whispers into my hair.

Silent tears are cascading down my cheeks, and he kisses them away, one by one.

"I...when will we see each other again?" I sob.

"Sooner than either of us expects," he says, like he knows something I don't.

I assume that his faith is a little stronger than mine, because I am a basketcase at the moment.

"I have something for you, but you can't open it until you are on the plane to Seattle." He hands me a gift bag.

"Same with yours—don't open it until you are on the plane."

We both stand there for what feels like hours. I have a death grip on his fingers.

Then he glances up toward town. "I better get going."

He reaches out to me, squeezing me tight into a hug. When he pulls back, I realize that I'm not the only one crying.

"Melody..." He leans in to kiss me on the cheek.

It's heavenly.

"I love you," he whispers in my ear.

My heart flutters. Sound the trumpets! Sing the "Hallelujah Chorus"!

Jude loves me!

"I love you, too!" I manage to choke out. He pulls back, and I can look into his eyes.

They echo the words that he just told me.

Silently, strongly, Jude pulls away from my gaze and walks

away, leaving with me his heart. I watch him go, until I can no longer see his figure.

I walk slowly back to the hotel, crying happy tears.

God, please protect Jude, Lord, please keep him, may Your grace shine upon him, and may You knit our hearts together in love. May we follow Your will every day and keep You first in our relationship, whatever it may be. God...please let us love.

Ros is waiting for me when I get back, her arms wide open. She too is crying, probably because she feels every ounce of my pain and sorrow.

But she also feels my happiness.

"Ros...he said he loves me." I weep into her shoulder.

"We both knew that he did." She comforts me, and after a minute, I am able to breathe.

"He loves me."

This time she laughs. "Yes, you mentioned that."

I smile. He loves me.

Forever.

13

"It's real—yes, it's real love…"
JOHN LENNON

Ros and I must be the two most idiotic people in the world, because we spend two days in Dallas and don't leave the hotel room. Yes, I know, we will probably live to regret it later, but we never really had a lot of "girl time" during the entire vacation, so we pretty much spend it lounging and watching chick flicks on cable.

We were both surprised, though, when on our first night in the city, Ros's cell phone rings. (Now that we can turn them on, for our fear of international roaming charges has subsided.)

It was Jason.

She was pleasantly surprised, and blushing, if I may add.

I haven't heard from Jude, but it's understandable. He has a lot to do. I still can't believe that he decided to quit the music industry. But like I mentioned, I'm sure he'll be back.

I was able to talk to Allie on the phone last night. It was weird, and I feel really bad for leaving her behind, especially because, in ways, she's gotten closer to me than Ros has. That aside, I was able to tell her all about my little romantic excursion.

She asked me a question that is still floating in my mind: "You mentioned that you love him, and he loves you, so are you going to get married?"

I told her we only would, or could, if it was in God's will, but honestly? I don't know. Despite falling in love with Jude in two weeks, I really don't know him well enough to marry for at least a year, right? Because I know him, but not deeply, no matter how much it feels like we have known each other for our entire lives.

But now Ros and I are sitting in a cab on the way to the airport, our heads stuck out the window in silence. We're reminiscing. Leaving the island was bad enough, but we're going home now. Did I mention that I don't really want to go home? It's like leaving will make this all feel like a dream, but it wasn't a dream! I honestly don't know how to explain it, but I want something to be true.

I haven't opened Jude's present. He said on the plane home to Seattle, and that's why I am fingering the package right now. It's nothing special, but I can't tell by the box or the weight what is inside.

I wonder if Jude has opened my book yet, or the stone? I wonder if he waited, too, until he is on his final destination (not that either of us really knew where that was going to be…I asked him, and he said he would let God lead him to where He thought he should go).

Whatever Jude got me, I will love it with every piece of my heart, just like I love him. Wherever he goes, whatever he does, I have to trust in God that He will bring us together in the end, because I really can't possibly think of living my life without him.

And it's only been two weeks.

Only two weeks.

Didn't I mention to you how I thought that "the one" would be the first guy to pass the two-week rule? Today would be exactly two weeks from the time I ran into Jude in the hallway and knocked all of his towels over. According to my plan, providing we don't break up in 24 hours, that means Jude is "the one."

Ros and I arrive at the airport and get out of the cab. We both stare straight ahead, like we'll do this even if it kills us. I know she said she doubted that she and Jason would write, but after the starstruck look in her eyes when he called, I have a feeling Ros has just found her very first boyfriend. Good for her!

I have hopefully found my very last boyfriend.

"Ready?" Ros grabs my elbow, and we walk into the airport together.

It doesn't take long to check our luggage, grab our carry-ons, and go through security. All the way here, Ros and I were in first class. This time, we are in economy and there are three seats. I'm sure I'm going to end up next to an overweight guy who talks too much, hasn't showered, and is probably one of those guys who tries to hit on the flight attendant. It's just what I need to top off the depressing end of a wonderful vacation.

"Wow. We're going home. It feels like we have been gone forever!" Ros looks dreamily out the window.

"It's almost like we are two different people going home than we were coming here. I can't wait to start my next novel. It's definitely going to be a romance based on a beach. There's nothing in comparison."

Ros chuckles. "And you know that I'll read it, cover to cover, in under four hours, tops."

Okay, maybe we really aren't that different than we were when we arrived. Except a little more tan, thank goodness. I didn't want to come back from vacation being white.

As we board the plane, I realize something.

It's February. It's going to be freezing cold in Washington.

Luckily, it's chilly here, and I'm already wearing a sweater.

February also means that I am going to be 20 in less than a month! With all of the excitement, I haven't even begun to think about what it means. College, I suppose. I called my parents and they said that I have been accepted, so it looks like I start there in about three weeks for the beginning of Winter Semester. That also means I'll probably have to get my job back to help pay for expenses. So I'll be going to school, writing a novel, and working part-time, with two best friends and a long-distance boyfriend.

Hmmm. I need a cat, too.

We stow our overhead luggage and settle into our seats, Ros with the window seat this time.

"Aren't you going to open that?" Ros looks down at my hands where my present from Jude is.

"You're right, I should. I can't take the suspense any longer!"

I rip open the package. There's a letter on top of tissue paper. I really want to dig underneath the paper to get whatever is below, but my parents have always taught me that it is polite to open the card first.

Miss Melody,

I am sad that I am leaving you, but know that we will be together very, very soon. I know this may be a little forward, but I love you, and I want you to know that every day, without any doubt, and to have a constant reminder of my devotion to you. This is my promise to you.

Okay, now I am curious. Pushing back the tissue paper, I reveal a little black velvet box. I open it up and—

There's nothing inside. I look at Ros, because I'm really confused. Did he forget to put the ring in? It was a ring, wasn't it?

And why is Ros looking at something over my head?

"I had to put it on for you." A deep, rich, amazing, British accent speaks from the aisle right behind me.

I spin (as much as you can do in a plane seat) to see the one true love of my life, Jude, standing with a beautiful white gold ring in his hand. No diamonds, of course, just a plain promise ring.

I love it.

But, unfortunately, I am too shocked to speak.

Jude, ever the comedian, looks at his ticket stub. "I think this is my seat, eh?" He tucks his carry-on overhead and plops down on the seat next to me, acting like that moment didn't just happen.

Then he turns and stares at me with those eyes that have held me captive in my dreams. "Melody Rebekah Kennedy, I love you, and I would like you to wear this ring as a token of my love and honor and commitment to you. Although I know it is not in our near future, I would also like to consider this ring as a promise from me to marry you when God reveals that the timing is right."

"Okay," I squeak and hold out my left hand. Jude gently picks it up and brushes a soft kiss on my ring finger before sliding the ring on. Engraved simply on the ring in script is the word *forever*.

That little voice in my head must have been talking to Jude the whole time.

Before I know what is happening, Jude leans toward me and kisses me with all the love and passion that I think is available to a man of any sort.

I am out of breath. "Jude." I stop him because I am happy, but way too confused at the moment.

"Yes, Miss Melody?"

"What are you doing here?"

He grins that crooked grin, and I know he's been a bad boy.

"Oh, didn't I tell you? I've decided on what college I want to go to. Unfortunately, that means I have to move into a small, boring town somewhere in Washington State. I wonder if I know anyone who lives there."

I am shell-shocked.

I can only do what any logical girl in my position would do.

I smack him.

Hard.

And then I kiss him.

Harder.

About the Author

JEN MELLAND is addicted to coffee, chocolate, and all things The Beatles. While *Melody* is far from being autobiographical, she was blessed enough to marry her own real love at 19. He was the first person she ever dated who lasted past the "two-week rule"!

Jen lives in Washington State with her amazing husband and family.

www.oaktara.com

Hopeful Romances for Hopeless Romantics.

Unforgettable romances that will make you fall in love again...
or for the first time. Available in Contemporary, Historical,
Prairie, Amish, Western, and other flavors.

Happily Ever After
SERIES

Who doesn't dream of happily ever after?

The Happily Ever After series highlights three contemporary women who are searching for their love-of-a-lifetime, complete with unconditional love, heart-warming acceptance, and toe-tingling romance.

Melody goes on her dream vacation trip and finds her dream guy—someone who is truly all she has ever hoped for, and more. But a surprising secret pulls them apart until she comes to a stunning realization that will transform her heart...and change her life forever.

Larkspur, fed up with dating losers and short on time while juggling several jobs, finds herself on a whirlwind ride of dates she allows her meddling mama to set up. Yet her heart is strangely tugged toward the neighbor who has driven her crazy all her life.

Evie is already in love with the man she's sure she's going to marry. But Ben is not her parents' choice. When they push her to consider an arranged marriage with Eli, their handsome family lawyer, which man will Evie choose? Is it possible to find the man you truly love while you're dating another?

All three women discover that true love doesn't always match what you plan, and it can be in a form much different from what you've imagined, but it can be better than you could ever dream.

Larkspur

KELSEY KILGORE

HAPPILY EVER AFTER

Would you let your mama pre-screen guys for you to date? Larkspur is just desperate enough to try it.

Larkspur—a twentysomething, freckle-faced Texan—has had enough of dating geeky, weird guys. So when her sociable mama suggests she pre-screen some guys for Lark to date, Lark's desperate enough to say yes. After all, with her three low-level jobs and the classes she's taking, she's not likely to snag *The Someone* anytime soon. But with her mama's Man Getting Project, she might have a chance at true love.

When Brant Stephens, her old classmate who lives down the street, tells her she resembles a sick cat in the midst of her parade of dates, she chalks it up to him being the most boring, mean, and predictable man on earth. He's got more degrees than she can remember, more annoying personality flaws than she can count, and all the gorgeous, shallow dates he could ever need. So why does he feel led to insult her every chance he gets? And why does she feel a strange flutter when he gazes at her with "that look"?

A fun, folksy romance
that will make you fall in love again…or for the first time.

"Why don't you meet guys at school or at your jobs, again?"

This is only the hundredth time Mama's asked me this. She doesn't know that I *am* highly motivated to meet someone. *The Someone,* if you will. So motivated that I secretly scan the personals from time to time, but there's no need to confess that to her, or to anyone else.

"You need help meeting quality men. *Pre-screened* men. So I'm going to screen men for you, and that way you'll only have to go out with the ones I approve first. I'll weed out the creeps."

"How nice." And, in theory, it does sound nice. But in the reality playing out in my head, *Oh, God help me….*

A Sneak Peek at *Larkspur*

1

"You want me to cut your hair?" Mama checks her reflection in the mirror, sucking in her cheeks to create the illusion of cheekbones.

"Why would I want you to do that? You don't even know how!" I remind her. She has apparently tired of watching me repeatedly blow a too-long strand off my forehead.

"Could if I tried," she says.

I doubt it, but it's just hair. "Sure."

Mama goes to the kitchen drawer and gets a pair of scissors I saw her cut raw chicken with last week. I don't say anything, though, because chicken germs probably don't hang around for a week anyway. And it's just hair.

I sit on the toilet and watch pieces of strawberry blond fall to the beige linoleum.

"I have a plan I need to tell you about."

I wish she didn't have scissors in her hands. Mama gets wild plans. That she's telling me about one while cutting, and that she needs to tell me about this one—well, neither one of those is good.

"Sure."

"I read in the newspaper that Plains Point has twice the available men your age as they do young women. I can't remember why that is, but that's what it said."

"Uh-huh." I doubt her statistic is correct but don't bother to say so.

"Men should be scrambling to get dates then."

"Haven't seen any scramble my way in a long time, Mama."

"I know! That's my point, baby."

Yeah, I'm 26, but Mama still calls me that. I think it's cute, really. Better than my real name.

"So…your plan?" I'm cringing, partly because the scissors are dull, and she's having to saw a little with them.

"Why don't you meet guys at school or at your jobs, again?"

This is only the hundredth time Mama's asked me this. She doesn't know that I *am* highly motivated to meet someone. *The Someone,* if you will. So motivated that I secretly scan the personals from time to time, but there's no need to confess that to her, or to anyone else.

"Mama, I do meet guys. But the ones who ask me out aren't believers, or if they are, they're creepy, and I always say no."

"Okay, so you need help meeting quality men. *Pre-screened* men."

"Uh-huh." I shift on the blue fuzzy toilet seat cover. "Would have been good to have a personal Man Screener that day."

"Exactly! I have more free time than you do, and I know how to meet men."

"You what?"

"How do you think I met Stanley?"

"Oh, right." Stanley is Mama's second husband—a real sweetheart who is so quiet I tend to forget him. But he's a good guy, I'll give her that.

"Sit still, and lean your head this way a little. So I'm going to screen men for you, and that way you'll only have to go out with the ones I approve first. I'll weed out the creeps."

"How nice." And, in theory, it does sound nice. But in the reality playing out in my head, *Oh, God help me.* Mama sending me the door-to-door vacuum salesman, or the guy at the bank who insists on sending me lollipops through the cash carrier. Or every single guy she talks to in the course of her day—and Mama talks to everybody. I can just hear it now: "Lark, I set up a date for you with the guy who held open the door for me at the post office." Oh, it could happen like that. Easily, knowing Mama.

Mama smiles at me. "I hoped you'd go for it."

"Um, do you think many will pass your screening? I mean, you can be pretty particular." Really, I'm afraid she'll overlook every single guy I'd actually like and send me on dates with all the ones I'd never consider. I can totally see her setting me up with losers by the herd, but rejecting all the hundreds of attractive, available men mentioned in the newspaper article.

"Well, that makes it that much better for you." Mama stops and checks her reflection again in the mirror. She turns her head slightly to each side, then returns to me with the scissors. "I won't pass anyone on to you that I wouldn't want for a son-in-law. What other qualities are you looking for?"

"Believer, denomination unimportant, but must have a very low creep factor, regardless of spiritual belief."

"Good one. Okay, how cute does he have to be?"

"I don't think that matters much. I don't think I'm too cute myself, right now, Mama." But I've always been such a dork over the really cute ones. Then I find out that they're flamingly gay or greatly conceited—with good reason, of course. Given the correct circumstances, I could totally be a fool for Tom Cruise, Scientology and all. Poor Katie, she really needed Mama. Blinded by cuteness, we can all go *so* wrong.

Which reminds me to ask how wrong my hair has gone. "You about ready to stop cutting?"

Mama steps back and looks at me, and I can tell it hasn't gone how she envisioned. "Well, maybe I should. I'd pictured a haircut that Ashley Judd had in the movie I watched last night, but this isn't it."

Oh, my gosh. If I'd known that, I would have stopped her. I look like a bad Peter Pan. Hair is hacked and sticking up in various lengths all over my head. If I were Ashley Judd, or any other Hollywood actress, maybe I could pull it off. Well, no, not even then. But I'm a freckle-faced Texas girl with too many jobs, and this haircut has the words *white trash* written all over it.

I sigh. "Thanks, Mama."

"It's just hair, baby."

Sure. Just hair. Like there weren't a half-dozen magazine articles on how to have hair like Katie Holmes in the weeks leading up to Tom's Eiffel tower proposal. Just hair.

"Yeah, find me a man who doesn't care about pretty hair. Maybe one of those guys who really thinks Sinead O'Connor is hot. Are there any of those guys?"

"Maybe in the nineties, there were. But I'll be sure to ask all the men I meet." She's kidding, so I try to ignore it. That would be easy, except that I can actually see her asking random men if they're more attracted to Julia Roberts or to Sinead O'Connor. I plant a kiss on her plump cheek and rush out the door for a shift at the Laun-dro-matio. It's completely lame, but I get to study a lot while I'm there, and I'm never behind on my laundry.

I can't help but note that my mother managed to diminish my physical appearance, while at the same time, plan how to get me a man. Interesting approach, I'll give her that. My cell phone rings, and it's her, even though I'm barely out of the driveway.

No hello. "I need to know what nights each week you can keep free for this project."

The Man Getting Project, I assume. "Wednesday and Friday."

"Don't you have singles class at church on Wednesdays?"

"No, they were a bad influence on me." I never bothered to explain that the singles class was far more interested in dating one another than in anything having to do with God. And, really, that could be a good thing considering I need someone to date...except it wasn't. Nothing like going to church and feeling like you've done something worse for your spiritual self than if you'd stayed home and played Cake Mania for hours on your laptop. I don't need that kind of guilt.

"Okay, Lark, I love you and don't you worry about what you look like."

"Thanks, Mama. I...wasn't." But now I am. I hang up, reaching for my slightly wavy spikes. Even Meg Ryan couldn't pull this look off.

Ross nods in acknowledgment, glad to see me so that he can leave the Laun-dro-matio. He is wearing all black, as usual, and his nose piercing looks different today, but I can't tell why.

"I like the hair. It's punker than I thought you were."

"Yeah, but not punker than Mama."

He looks at me like he doesn't understand what I said and waves with two fingers as he leaves. The place is empty, so I spread out my books and sit on one of the big folding tables.

I've been there long enough to have a cramp in my neck when Brant Stephens walks by. I roll my eyes at the khakis and denim shirt he wears, extra starch.

We went to school together—elementary, not college. Brant has more degrees than I can remember and more annoying personality flaws than I can count. He lives down the street, on the other side, and he sometimes runs in the mornings when I do. It's an unfortunate occurrence, and on those mornings we exchange a few insults when we pass—a game that used to be more fun.

He thinks I'm nobody, and I think he's an overrated somebody. He had scholarships and tuition handed to him, and I can't blame him for not being able to relate to me. I work two low-paying jobs—three if you count my living arrangements. I do yardwork and errands for my landlady, and in return I pay a very low rent for the one-bedroom apartment in her backyard.

Besides working at the Laun-dro-matio, I work at the campus bookstore. I am the Minimum Wage Queen, and no job is beneath me. I kind of like that about me, actually.

I've taken classes for too many years at the local community college and have no intention of earning a degree. I simply take the courses I think I might need one day, regardless of how they fit into a degree plan. Which isn't smart, especially since I've been harboring a secret desire to become an accountant. But it sounds so dull, and so not me that I'm in denial of it. I think of myself as more lively than any accountant could ever be, so I hesitate in rushing in that direction. I consider myself more of a firefighter, or private detective sort. Not that those jobs appeal to me, but they possess the "glam quality" that accounting doesn't have.

I've finished kneading the knots out of my neck when Brant sticks his head in the door. I was hoping he wouldn't. He's been at the dry cleaners next door and has an armful of clear-bagged preppie clothes.

"Hey, Lark, you looked like you were dragging a little this morning. Feeling out of shape?"

"Nah, only a little short on sleep." I don't attempt to return the slam, since I know he's going to notice my hair any minute. This is not an insult-fest I can win, so I play sweet.

He steps inside and lets the door shut behind him with a bang. "Hey, do you remember that cat I had when we were younger? The one with the skin disease that made her scratch all the time?"

I remember. "Yeah."

"That's what you remind me of today, Lark. Her fur stood up just like that."

I have no comeback. I can't even play sweet anymore. I smile, sort of, and look at the door. My neck tenses up again.

Something flashes across his face, and I think he's about to apologize. Even that was meaner than our usual exchanges. He smiles back, showing his perfect teeth, and walks out. No apology. The door bangs closed, and I watch him carefully hang his preppie clothes on the hook in the back of his silver Mercedes.

That has to be the most boring, predictable man on earth. Then again, they said that about BTK, and he turned out to be a serial killer. Brant couldn't even have a surprising side to his personality, much less a dangerous one. And this is why for at least the last five years I've thought of him as Boring Brant.

I stare blankly at my books, depressed at the thought of resembling anybody's out of shape, sick cat, now long dead. Any flicker of hope that I might, with Mama's help, be on the verge of meeting *The Someone* totally vanishes. I am ill-suited to attract anyone at all if I remind Brant of that particular cat. His cat easily made the one in *Sweet Home Alabama* look healthy. You know, the one that had been set on fire and survived a few explosions? The worst part is that he wasn't only being mean. I remember that cat, and there is a frightening similarity.

Hours pass with that thought in the back of my mind as I sit alone in the Laun-dro-matio. I'm studying a chapter on tax laws for my current accounting course, which I've found doesn't require all of my brain to be present anyway. Maybe I'll become a brilliant accountant in a country in which a woman's hair is unimportant, and the locals find it a highly exciting, glamorous career.

It's nice to see Gloria, who has the next shift, since her arrival means I can walk out into the bright evening, instead of sitting behind glass.

There's something about this part of West Texas, even in March, that makes the evening sun turn everything golden and pretty, so it's good to be out here. This square of businesses is my very small world. The Laun-dro-matio sits on one side, with the dry cleaners next door, and that side faces the florist shop, Rosie's

Posies, and the Save-Some grocery store. On another side of the square are the Coffee Café—café mochas that rival Starbucks and are way cheaper—and Hazel's Hair Haven. I've never been to Hazel's, but she's probably better than Mama.

There are other businesses that open and close after a couple of months, and I don't keep tabs on those. Two blocks behind the Coffee Café is where I live, in Mrs. Huttle's backyard apartment. She's a grouch of an old woman, and she likes me to do what she wants without having to speak to me. Mind-reading required for that role.

I head to Coffee Café for a café mocha but never get there. A woman standing outside Hazel's Hair Haven stamps out a cigarette, and when I pass her, she reaches out to touch my elbow. I jump. I didn't expect that.

"Hi there." She's holding my arm and looking at my hair, and I am suddenly back in the hallway of elementary school and a teacher is trying to determine if I have a hall pass. I decide these dynamics are unacceptable and reach out and hold her by the elbow, too. It would have been better to pull away, but this lady is almost as big as Mama, and I don't think I'd get away if she didn't want me to. So now we're just strangers, standing there in a weird half embrace, and that's not what I was going for either.

Still holding her arm, I say, "Hi."

She shrugs me off with ease, opens the door to Hazel's, pulling me in, while never taking her eyes off my hair. "Honey, it looks like you got attacked by some really dull-bladed pruning shears. I'm Hazel, and I will help you." She's talking slowly, as if to an accident victim about to go into shock. And she thinks that is clearly the appropriate state of mind for someone with hair like mine.

"Okay, Hazel. They were my mama's kitchen shears, and you can help me, but I don't have any money on me today."

"You don't have to pay me—this is my good deed for society, honey."

I'm in her blue vinyl chair, and I start to ask if she wants to know what I'd like it to look like when she's done, but I don't. There are probably not a lot of options left anyway.

Hazel snips away, muttering about kitchen shears, too involved in her mission for small talk. Which is fine with me. Despite my being grabbed on the sidewalk, Hazel is kind of nice, and I decide that her heart must be very giving, to go to so much trouble for a stranger. Just then she starts cursing, having found a particularly short patch. Well, you can have a mouth like a sailor and still have a giving heart, I suppose.

"This here?" She points to the patchy part behind my left ear, and I nod in acknowledgment. "Only time can heal this, honey."

Isn't that a lyric from a Cher song?

"You come back when it grows out, and I'll even it out for you." She shakes her head from side to side, continuing her work. I wonder if small talk is only for paying customers, or if Hazel even does small talk. This is such a far cry from the beauty parlor scenes in *Steel Magnolias,* but it doesn't matter. I look so much more fabulous than I thought I could with short hair and a patchy spot. Short wisps of strawberry blond decorate my head, and I am so glad Hazel grabbed me. I am chic and sophisticated and modern, except that it's still just me. However, it's pretty hot, considering what it looked like an hour ago.

"You work around here, don't you?" Hazel asks.

I fill her in on my jobs, and she gives me a pat. "Good for you. A hard worker. I like that. You come see me when you need a trim, and if you ever need another job."

I look around the deserted place, wondering if Hazel needs any help. But I thank her anyway and even give her a hug. She laughs and follows me out to light another cigarette and maybe accost another worthy pedestrian.

I grab the phone on the second ring as I carefully tiptoe across the carpet to avoid getting carpet fuzz on my pedicure. After arriving home, I checked Hazel's amazing repair work for the third time in the mirror and painted my toenails Pink Kiss.

"Hey, Lark, can I come over?"

It's Christine, long-time friend and fellow nail-polish enthusiast—which we regularly trade. "Sure."

"Great, I need help putting together a jogging stroller."

Christine is my age and single, and this makes no sense. "Is there something you want to tell me?"

"Yeah, I got a job! See ya in a minute!"

And she hangs up without explaining why she's putting together a jogging stroller, or even what that might be.

I meet her out in front of Mrs. Huttle's, and we haul in parts and tools together, making it in one trip.

"So this is for what?"

"You know Marilyn, the lady I babysit for sometimes? She's pregnant with her second kid, and her doctor put her on bedrest."

"Uh huh. And this is hers?" I put the stroller pieces on the step in front of my door, noting that it isn't completely unassembled. This is a good thing, or we'd be at it for hours.

"Yeah, her 'extra.' Marilyn was the StrollerMama instructor, but she can't be now, of course."

"What's a StrollerMama instructor?"

"You know, those moms who meet at parks and at the mall and do workouts as a group, and they all have their kids in strollers."

"So you're the new StrollerMama?" I laugh at her. Hard.

"Yes! What's so funny?"

"You're not a mom, and I bet this is the closest you ever came to a stroller."

"So? I did aerobics at the Y one summer! I can instruct a bunch of moms to walk, while doing knee lifts, and encourage proper breathing."

"Sure. You're right, you can."

Christine flips her long, straight brown ponytail behind her shoulder. "And I'll be really positive. I plan on quoting Scriptures to them pertaining to motherhood. Like, 'Your children shall rise up and call you blessed.' "

"Good luck with that."

Christine is making great headway on stroller assembly, and I wonder why she thought she needed my help in the first place.

"Next week you can decide to be a midwife if this doesn't work out."

I hand her a tube-shaped part and she asks, "What's Mama up to?"

"Finding me a man."

"Gooood! If anyone can, it's her. Sorry, didn't mean it like that."

"It's fine. I've been thinking the same thing. Don't you think, though, that it'll be tough?"

"No, why?"

"Maybe I've been watching too much TV or flipping through too many *People* mags, but I'm pretty sure great hair and boobs are still 'in.' "

"Uh huh." Christine reaches for a part, and I scoot it closer with my foot.

"So, in today's society, these are the appropriate man-getting tools. In case you haven't noticed, I don't have them. How in the world are you supposed to get a guy without hair and boobs, when every other woman out there has them and flaunts them?"

"What about Kate Hudson?"

"Gorgeous, and gorgeous hair, if not the rest."

"What about attracting just one man? *The* man? I mean, why do you need to attract all kinds of guys, when you're only looking for one?"

I hesitate before asking, "How can you attract even one, if his tongue is falling out of his mouth and his eyes are glazed over by all the cleavage on everyone else? Every single commercial, TV show, and magazine can't be wrong when they indicate that breasts are still all the rage, and of great importance to your average joe." I look down at my chest and back at Christine. "Did you ever watch that show?"

"What show?" Christine isn't known for her attention span.

"*Average Joe.*"

"No."

"Oh. It was okay. Not as trashy as a lot of reality TV."

I raise my eyebrows, waiting to see if she'll remember what we're talking about. She spins a wheel with her foot. "But you don't want your 'average joe.' God will make you absolutely irresistible to The One. You know, set you apart in a way that can't be missed. And it won't be hard. You're too pretty to be talking like this."

"Yeah. I'll look like those early religious paintings. When the artists wanted to show that their representation of Jesus was the true Christ, they'd paint a yellow half circle behind his head, like a bright firefly was always buzzing behind him. You know the paintings I mean?"

"Right. You think God will give you a firefly glow?"

"No, I'd rather He give me breasts, but I don't think that's happening, suddenly, at age 26, either."

"Sarah thought she was too old, and look what happened to her." Christine gives me a knowing look.

I can't think of any Sarah that we know, but Christine won't stop with the knowing, nodding look. And then, because it's Christine and I understand her weird mind, I get it. And that's the only reason. "*Sarah?* As in the woman who had Isaac at, like, age 100? *That's* who you're comparing me to?"

"No! Not at all. Well, yeah, but I didn't think it through first."

Christine giggles as only she can. It makes her sound like she's five, with a secret. "I know!" Christine stares at me. Clearly she has a great idea. "What about a Miracle Bra?"

Ah, and this just shows how much she doesn't get my predicament. "Christine, I'm *wearing* a Miracle Bra!"

"*Really?* Huh." And she can't help but laugh, and I don't blame her.

"You about done with that?"

"Yeah, you've been an amazing help," she says sarcastically. "What happened to your hair anyway? It's cute."

"Mama cut it. Then a lady grabbed me on the street and fixed it so it didn't look so bad."

"Yeah, sure, Lark." She doesn't believe me, but I let it go.

"Pray for me tomorrow, and I'll call and tell you how it goes." She walks off with her newly assembled jogging stroller, doing high knee lifts.

"You go, Mom!"

I was going to give her Pink Kiss to take home, but my phone rings and Mama sounds out of breath on the other end. "Larkspur!"

I hate it when she calls me that.

"I have two fantastic men who are meeting you for coffee tonight. Meet Jason at 7 o'clock at Coffee Café, and meet Jim right after that at 7:30."

"Tonight?" How in the world did she meet two fantastic men since lunchtime? I've never met two fantastic men, well, ever. I wonder what Mama's version of fantastic men is. An image of Stanley, my stepfather, in his one-piece, belted work suit comes to mind. Hmm. And she met *two* this quickly?

"Yes, tonight. You said you were free on Wednesdays and Fridays, and today is Wednesday."

"I know, but I didn't think you meant *now!*"

"Well, it worked out that way, baby. And wear a skirt. You have my legs, you know." *Click.*

I wonder at that combination of advice. Mama has legs like tree trunks. Like hundred-year-old redwoods that cars could drive through because they're so wide. And then the conflicting "so wear a skirt." Conflicting in the same way as giving me the sick-cat haircut and then announcing it's time to attract men. But that's Mama.

I run to the bathroom, because if I don't shave I'm going to have legs so furry they'll remind another man of his cat.

2

So I'm sitting in Coffee Café with incredible hair, hairless legs, and a skirt, fervently praying that the guy who walked in is my date. This is not your typical Plains Point guy. I've never seen guys who looked like this one except maybe in magazines or on TV. *Wow.* I know what it is: it's like the hottest guy ever, straight from the pages of the latest J.Crew catalog. No kidding. (And no, I don't shop J.Crew on my income, but I do like the catalogs.) Somehow, prayers are answered. J.Crew comes over and offers the most amazing lopsided smile and asks if I'm Lark.

"I am." It comes out all breathy. I'm so thankful Mama didn't tell him my name is Larkspur. I notice the five-ish shadow on his jawline is a few shades lighter than the dark, dark hair on his head.

Surprisingly, the chemistry is two-way. *Thank You, God, and thank you, Mama!*

J.Crew sits across from me, and we talk and laugh and stare. I hate it that he's the first of my two dates and that he's already said that he knows he only has 30 minutes with me. If he were the next guy, we'd be closing down Coffee Café. Somewhere about halfway through our half hour he nervously reaches across the table and places his hand next to mine, so some of our fingers are touching. He isn't holding my hand, but it's almost. It's pretty good, and I realize it's been such a long time since I've had a date that even a little finger brushing is nice....

At five the next morning I pull on shorts, for the sole reason that I happen to have hairless legs, a shirt, and shoes, and run out the door with extra energy. I'm halfway down the block when the Original Yuppie catches up to me.

"You in a hurry?" Brant calls.

"It's called running for a reason."

"You just seem faster today." He's keeping pace, looking down at me from my right side. He has on his usual running ensemble, the kind of weatherproof pants and jacket that swish with each step. I don't know why, but I like that sound.

"It's a great day, Brant," I say and turn up the speed, leaving him behind.

Fifteen minutes later we pass, on opposite sides of the street. Red-faced and out of breath, we're both too tired to talk, but I watch him watch me, and after I pass, I turn to see him running one way, still watching me with his head turned.

Poor guy. One day I look like a sick cat and the next I have cute hair, naked hairless legs, and the most flattering pair of shorts eBay ever had for a quarter plus shipping. And that whole "other men want me" energy—any girl knows that's potent stuff.

I accept J.Crew's—Jason's—hand gladly as he offers it to help me from his pickup. Not sure what to wear, I'd gone with a khaki skirt and blue button-down shirt with my favorite sandals—blue with bows. They are so girlie, I love them. With my curveless figure, I gladly take "girlie" anyway I can get it, even if it's only on footwear.

We walk into a school auditorium. I'm surprised at the hundreds of people already there and the flags everywhere—not one of them Texan. I'm a half step behind Jason and speed up to grab the hand he holds out again for me.

He lopsidedly smiles, and my heart flips. We scoot into a wooden bleacher seat just as a guy in a cowboy hat takes the microphone and talks about independence and freedom. I'm not listening, really, since Jason is still holding my hand and keeps looking at me with those amazing brown eyes. I wish we were somewhere else planning our future together. Maybe that's premature, or maybe I'm just a woman of vision.

There's periodic whooping and clapping and fist pumping, a lot like a Texas football game where the fans are into it. You don't have to know what's going on in the game to be supportive, so I whoop and fist-throw, too, and Jason beams and scoots closer. He had called this a rally when he invited me, and I'm only now wondering what that means.

"I'm so glad you understand," he says into my ear, and alarms ring distantly in my head. I ignore them, only thinking that I want him to say something else—anything else—into my ear again.

"Jason, I don't understand at all, but I'm having a great time!" I say into his ear.

He gives me a troubled look, and I try to reassure him by yelling, "Freedom!" with the crowd and flashing him a smile.

After a few minutes, there's a short break and people go around and clap each other on the back and shake hands—like at a church picnic, or at halftime at a high school football game.

Jason doesn't join in but turns to me. "Lark, this is my life, and I need you to understand it."

"So explain it to me! I think your life is a lot of fun!"

"I'm a Citizen of the Republic of Texas. Do you know what that means? Did you listen to anything I said to you the other night?"

How can I say that I was too busy staring at him? I say the first thing that sounds right. "I'm a citizen of Texas, too, Jason! Yea for us!" It comes out kinda wrong.

"*Not* a citizen of Texas. *Never that.* A citizen of the *Republic* of Texas. We're Separatists, Lark."

I lean closer, not wanting anyone to hear me ask what a Separatist is, so I ask in his ear.

He sighs, maybe angry that he has to explain it to me since I thought we were at a fun political pep rally of some sort. "Texas is an independent nation, and we fight peacefully against the occupationalist government of the United States. We accept all religions and races, despite what the media says about us."

"Did you say *occupationalist?*" Oh, is this the group that had a hostage situation several years back? Uh, yes, I think it is.

"Yes. Is this still 'fun'?" He's studying me, hoping I'll accept his answers.

I can't. No matter how cute he is—and he is *so* cute. Polished, yet still with a rugged look. A little Brad Pitt, when he's scruffy. *So* pretty, yet still edgy—but maybe that's only the whole cult thing he apparently has going on. Despite his prettiness, I can't accept his explanation. "I'm sorry. I voted for Bush! I'm a conservative Republican, and I *like* being part of the United States, Jason."

"We aren't part of the United States, whether you or anyone else recognize it or not!"

"Okay, in my world we are." I decide to speak calmly and slowly, but I can't think through what I should say that will get me out of this. "I know I'm in your world right now, but if you could drive me back to mine, I'd appreciate it."

This is the wrong thing to say, and Jason stands up and walks off, disappearing amongst the other, far less physically attractive Separatists.

Oh, God, help me. Forgive me! I have been lured by lust straight into the Texas underworld. Even the flags are different here.

The crowd seems less like a football bunch now, and I make my exit quickly, wishing I weren't wearing the blue sandals with bows that look great and kill my feet.

I'm two miles from home, which is two miles too far in these shoes. I laugh at the thought of me being a "woman of vision." Such a woman would not be stranded in these shoes, ever. I'm considering calling someone for a ride, but I'm not ready to share the details of this afternoon with anyone yet.

I've just stepped out of my sandals when a silver Mercedes slows down, stopping next to me. Boring Brant leans out the window, looking as neat and pressed as he always does.

"Need a ride, Larkspur?" he calls sweetly. He knows I don't like my name.

If I were in any other shoes, my answer would be no. But the asphalt is warm under my feet. Desperate, I force a smile. "Thanks." I hope he doesn't ask why I'm carrying my shoes. I am about to open the passenger door when I see a pretty redhead seated there. I smile at her and slide into the backseat.

She turns around and extends a hand to me, which I shake. "I'm Danica."

"Hi, I'm Lark. Thanks, Brant."

"No problem. What happened to you? Car break down or something?" He's being nice to me because of Danica, but I'm glad anyway.

"Uh, no. Just got…separated…from my ride."

"Oh, I hate it when that happens," Danica says, with what appears to be genuine sympathy.

"Who was your ride?" Brant catches my eye in the rearview mirror.

"No one you know, I'm sure."

"You know, there's a big Texas Independence rally going on back there…gee, that's not where you were, right, Lark?"

I sink lower in my seat.

"Lark?"

His tone is innocent and sweet, and so fake. I know it, but Danica doesn't. At the moment I can't stand this man. Or at any other moment. There was a short span of time in high school, though, but no one ever knew. I was hormonally imbalanced then, so it didn't count.

"Yes, Brant! That's where I was! I chanted for independence and freedom and even punched the air with my fist. Are you happy? *I* was a Separatist today."

He doesn't say anything, but I can feel his satisfaction the rest of the way to our street. When we get there, he pulls the car over, turns and smiles at me like he's holding back a giant laugh, and hits the automatic unlock button to release me.

Danica says, "I support *all* political views and believe they are separate but equal." She smiles.

Huh? I can picture her at a beauty pageant with the same smile proudly saying, "I support…world peace!"

"Wow, that's, um, nice, Danica. I decided to leave when I remembered they sometimes take hostages to prove their point. But that's just me." I smile insincerely at Brant as I put on my sandals. The thought of Brant with Danica helps me refrain from slamming his perfect, silver door.

Brant is a *bug*, I think, in true second-grader style. He's so great, he probably didn't even notice her beauty pageant looks. And hair! Can't forget the gorgeous, flowing locks of Disney-worthy hair. No, he was entranced at first glance by her endless compassion and tolerance of all "separate but equal" political views. Yeah, that's it!

It's not too hard to figure out why Brant's with the beautiful Danica, but the other way around? I don't know. She could have anyone, I bet.

I walk toward my house wondering what in the world she sees in a dope like Brant….

About the Author

KELSEY KILGORE makes her home in windswept West Texas with her three boys, two dogs, and one cat. She's the writer behind the award-winning blog *HolyMama,* candid reflections on her life and family. She appreciates small details and delights in bringing them to life in works of fiction, often with humor.

Whenever possible, she's lifting weights at the gym, off-roading in her big pickup, wakeboarding, kickboxing, or engaging in other exceptionally ladylike endeavors. Next on her list of activities to try are rappelling, parasailing, surfing, and possibly cooking. She is a fan of eBay, colorful shoes, fantastically designed jeans, and long candlelit baths.

http://holymama.org/ ▪ www.oaktara.com

HILARY HAMBLIN

HAPPILY EVER AFTER

Caught between the love of two men, how will she choose?

Evie's wealthy parents have just given her an ultimatum: stop dating her boyfriend Ben, or lose their financial support her junior year of college. Worse, they want her to consider an arranged marriage to the family lawyer, Eli Wheatly. True, Eli is handsome—tall, with a mop of curly black hair—but looks aren't enough for Evie. She dreams of true love.

When Evie and Ben hatch a scheme to continue quietly dating while she goes out on a few dates with Eli to keep her parents happy, Evie is surprised and confused by the romantic flutterings she feels around Eli. What if she's found the man she truly loves...while dating another?

A beautiful small-town romance
that will make you fall in love again...or for the first time.

falling in love
CONTEMPORARY

As Evie and Ben shared a long, sweet kiss, her heart ached at the news she had to tell him. Although she'd only been away from the university for two days, she had missed the taste of his mouth on hers and the smell of his freshly shaven skin. She nuzzled his cheek with her nose until he laughed and pushed her away. "Miss me?"

"Mm-hmm," he murmured as he took his turn nuzzling her neck with his nose until she giggled.

But when she gazed into his blue eyes, she remembered her unsavory task. "We have a problem," she confessed. "When I went home this weekend, Mom and Dad ambushed me. They don't think we should see each other anymore...."

"So we pretend to break up and then see each other secretly," Ben offered. "Nobody has to know. When your parents see how hurt and sad you are, they'll come to their senses. In the meantime, you'll have to start dating again."

Evie backed away until she held Ben at arm's length. "But I don't want to see anyone else."

"The idea of you dating some other guy drives me nuts. But your parents won't believe you're actually trying if you don't date. And it can't be just anyone. You have to go out with someone they choose."

Evie's thoughts slid back to the vision of Eli Wheatly, her family's new lawyer, sitting comfortably at the other end of the swing on her porch....

A Sneak Peek at *Evie*

1

"**D**on't fall in love..." Her mother's warning repeated over and over to Evie as she sat across the table from her parents.

They had approved of Ben Fisher as a fling Evie would outgrow, but not as a husband. Now, a year into her dating relationship with Ben, her parents were drawing the line. Evie had arrived home from the university an hour earlier with a bag full of dirty laundry and a backpack brimming with homework. Ben and his roommates had found a better apartment and were moving, so this weekend appeared to be the perfect time to visit her parents.

Yet as soon as she dropped her bags in the foyer, they called her into the dining room.

"It's not that we don't like Ben, honey. He's a nice guy," her mother droned on.

"But he's from a different world than you are. You have expectations and responsibilities to the family," her father added.

Evie squinted at her parents. They were doctors in a small town...not English royalty. What responsibilities did she have to anyone regarding the person she dated?

"You and Ben have been dating for some time, and we're concerned that things are getting too serious." Her mother folded her hands in front of her and glanced at Evie's father, as if signaling him to take a turn.

"So, from now on," her father announced, "if you want us to pay your sorority dues, car note, gas bill, restaurant tab, as well as…" He ticked off a list of Evie's most treasured possessions. "Then you will end this relationship before it goes too far." Her father looked her straight in the eye, his brows arched in expectation of an affirmative response from her.

"You've got to be kidding," she whispered, as the beginning of tears clouded her vision. "I'm twenty years old, I make good grades, and I'm graduating in just over a year. You can't tell me what to do."

Anger boiled inside, racing to heat her face. How dare they interfere in her life in such a manner! For years, her parents had allowed her a later curfew than most of her friends and paid off her credit cards whenever the bill came. They had never set restrictions on her before, so why start now?

However, neither smiled as they laid out their arrangement. They simply sat stoically, side by side, entrenched in their shared position.

She couldn't believe it. They had ambushed her. Evie grit her teeth to keep from screaming at them. Now the fact they'd both been home when she'd arrived made sense. Her mother and father were never home from work this early, and rarely did they spend a Friday evening together. That meant they must have been planning this discussion ever since she'd phoned earlier in the week to tell them she was coming home for the weekend.

"You're right," her father agreed. "But we also don't have to provide these extras for you. As you said, you are twenty years old. You can get a job and pay for these luxuries on your own."

Evie opened her mouth to respond, but words would not form.

Shock crept over her anger as she processed the reality of her father's statement. She'd never considered herself the spoiled princess type, because she worked hard for her grades and other achievements. But material matters rarely concerned her, since her parents had always taken care of whatever bills rolled through the mail slot.

Mentally, she quickly calculated how much she would need every month to continue living the way she was currently. The calculations easily reached $1500 a month. Where would she find a part-time job that would pay that much and still have time to continue her studies?

Then she thought of Ben. What would she tell him? He'd be crushed by the real reason they could no longer date. Could she pretend to be angry at him? Angry enough about something that she could break off their relationship without telling him the truth? Could she make such a scene even believable?

She pictured his face, and her heart ached at even the idea of hurting him so deeply.

Her mother touched Evie's arm gently. "You can think about it over the weekend and let us know what you decide before you leave on Sunday. I believe, after some time, you'll realize we are right. We love you, Evie," she murmured, "and we only want what's best for you."

Her father's keen eyes studied her. "While you are considering our agreement, we'd like you to join us for dinner tonight. The law firm we use turned our account over to a new lawyer, and he's coming by for dinner. Taylor and Leigh Anna will be joining us as well."

Evie's hope and resolve soared as she thought about her brother and his wife. Surely they wouldn't allow her parents to dictate her love life. They would see her side and help her challenge her parents' ultimatum. After all, she and Taylor had been partners in crime for years, and she had known Leigh Anna since kindergarten.

She was certain her parents had never given Taylor this kind of ultimatum.

She sighed inwardly. Then again, Taylor had never dated anyone seriously until Leigh Anna, and she was perfect. The petite, dark-haired girl with large brown eyes had captured her parents' hearts from the beginning. It didn't hurt that Leigh Anna's father owned the very profitable local funeral home or that she intended to become a nurse practitioner. She was a perfect fit for Evie's family.

So why had Evie been the one to fall for someone whose family was so unlike her own? She considered Ben's family even as she asked herself the question. What was wrong with them, in her parents' eyes?

Ben's mother and father had a happy marriage. He had three younger brothers, all of whom played sports and expected to pay for most of their college tuition through scholarships. Ben himself had been a talented baseball player on full scholarship until he damaged his shoulder.

Now he worked two jobs to save money so he could go to school every other semester. His education major might never make him a rich man, but he would have steady work with good benefits. Both of his parents were teachers, and his mom worked retail on the weekends and summers to pay for extras for the boys. They worked hard, owned a modest home, and drove late-model, although used, cars.

Maybe they were not as well off as Evie's own family, but they certainly did not crawl out of the gutter. Disgust grew as Evie mulled over her parents' prejudices. Worse, they'd left no room for discussion in the "arrangement."

She took a deep breath. "What time is supper?" she muttered as nicely as she could. She bit her lower lip to keep it from trembling. Emotional outbursts ranked just below poor on her parents' list of negative qualities in a person.

"Seven," her father informed her.

"Fine," Evie replied in an even tone. She pushed herself away from the table and, chin held high, walked back to the foyer to gather her things. Then, ascending the stairs, she hurried to her room and shut the door quickly, unable to resist a little slam. Dropping her bags on the floor, she threw herself on the bed and allowed sobs to take over until she could barely breathe.

When her emotion was spent, she scanned her room with tear-streaked vision. The late afternoon sunlight streamed through the gauzy pink curtains on her windows and cast shadows on the beige carpet.

A thought flickered. *Maybe I could sell something and come up with the money for my bills...at least for a little while.* But a swift inventory revealed only a few fairly expensive decorations. Even if she sold them all, she would probably only come up with $500.

Her eyes darted to the wooden jewelry box on her dresser. She jumped from her bed and landed in front of the box with two steps. Taking out several necklaces adorned with elegant, precious stones, she calculated what they might be worth. She could perhaps live a little more than a month, maybe two, on the proceeds.

Slipping her grandmother's diamond ring on her right hand, Evie admired it, turning it in the sunlight until it glittered.... No, she couldn't sell the ring. She couldn't give up a precious heirloom for a month's rent.

The clock on her nightstand caught her attention. With slumped shoulders, she temporarily abandoned the search of her earthly possessions in favor of a much-needed shower before dinner.

An hour later Evie gathered her silky blond hair into a twist on top of her head and secured it with a shimmering blue barrette that matched the color of her eyes. She allowed a few strands to fall around her face and made a mental note to hit them with the curling iron before dinner. Twisting first to the left and then to the right, she swished her dress, a blue and brown swirled pattern, around her legs. Tiny straps accented the remains of her summer tan. A matching blue sweater lay on the end of her bed to keep her warm on the cool September evening.

After checking the time, she headed into her bathroom to make fast work of curling her stray hairs and dusting sweet loose powder over her face.

A pro at attending her parents' dinner parties after many years, she knew she had to look her best, for she'd be on display. Taylor, her brother, would be expected to discuss politics with the new lawyer, and Evie would be expected to look beautiful and smile incessantly. As angry as she was with her parents, Evie had no desire to humiliate them.

Straightening her shoulders, she walked out of her room and down the stairs, carefully adjusting her sweater.

Voices already sounded from the foyer. Adopting her public face, she reached the landing and stepped into view of the foyer.

"Here she is," her mother announced in a welcoming tone. "Eli Wheatly, this is our daughter, Evelyn."

Evie stopped. Her muscles tensed. The tall, dark-headed man in his early thirties who stood before her beamed a white, sparkling smile her way. His slick black suit nearly matched his mop of curly black hair.

"Mom?" she questioned as she cast a weak smile toward the stranger and darted an incredulous look at her mother.

"Evelyn, don't be rude," her mother chided teasingly. "Come down here. Eli is the new lawyer handling our account."

No. It can't be...

Evie stifled a scream and walked numbly down the rest of the stairs. "Nice to meet you," she managed to choke out.

"Very nice to meet you, Evelyn," he replied, still smiling.

"It's *Evie*. Only my parents call me *Evelyn*," she murmured through clenched teeth.

"Evie, why don't you show Eli to the living room?" her mother prompted. "Taylor and Leigh Anna are already waiting there with your father. Dinner will be ready in a minute."

Evie's mother exited in the opposite direction toward the kitchen, leaving Eli and Evie alone in the foyer. After an awkward moment, Evie swallowed hard and led the way to the living room.

"Your mom tells me you are a junior political science major," Eli said as he followed Evie through the house.

Evie nodded, refusing to speak even though she knew Eli was innocent in her parents' scheme. As the shock wore off, though, Evie's anger toward her parents grew.

For a second, the fire she imagined shooting from her eyes to her father did just that as she and Ben entered the living room.

Her father returned her glare with one of warning.

She seethed inwardly. How could they insist she end her relationship with Ben one minute and in the next breath throw her together with someone else?

Evidently Eli's parents are closer to the right caliber than Ben's, she told herself.

But Evie cared little about Ben's—or Eli's—work or parents' position in society. Her focus turned from finding a way to stay together with Ben to merely surviving the evening without embarrassing herself any more than her parents already had.

"Taylor!" she exclaimed, trying to hide her anger.

Her brother crossed the room to hug his younger sister. He shared Evie's blond hair and blue eyes but had their father's tall, stocky frame. Thin metal glasses framed his eyes, giving his clean-shaven face a studious look. "Evie, Dad said you were home this weekend. How are classes?"

"Same as ever. Are you going to Homecoming next month?"

Taylor shrugged. "Don't know. Guess it depends on the weather. You know I'm not big on the whole reunion thing. I keep in touch with some of my frat brothers. That's enough for me."

"Taylor," his father protested, "you have to go to Homecoming. You can make a lot of good contacts through the alumni you'll meet."

Taylor rolled his eyes after he'd stepped out of his father's line of vision.

Evie stifled a giggle. "Come on, Taylor, it'll give you a chance to catch up with Ben."

From the corner of her eye, Evie caught a second look of warning from her father. Triumphant in her little dig, Evie smiled at her brother and moved past him to sit next to Leigh Anna.

"How's the nursing program going?" she asked, changing the subject and leaving Eli to talk to her father and brother.

Leigh Anna's dark eyes sparkled as she discussed the new procedures she'd learned that week and how much she enjoyed clinicals.

Evie half listened to her sister-in-law as her brain churned with ways to get out of entertaining her parents' lawyer all night. Just skipping out crossed her mind, but even in her present state, her conscience wouldn't allow such a plan. Right as Leigh Anna finished her discourse on nursing school, Evie's mother announced dinner had been served in the dining room.

Evie lagged behind the crowd, her heels clicking on the brick floor as she studied her mother's table arrangement. A white tablecloth covered the antique cherry table and almost blended with her mother's white china. Only the platinum rim around the dishes set them apart.

Everyone found a place around the table as soon as they entered the room, leaving only one open spot for Evie—next to Eli. She smiled politely as she approached her chair. Eli smiled in return and stood to pull her chair out from the table for her.

She stared at him in disbelief. Eli was not her date, yet even on their most romantic evenings Ben had never pulled her chair out from the table for her.

Ben... Her thoughts drifted to the man she loved so deeply, the man her parents were making an obvious attempt to replace.

"Evie," her father called from his place at the head of the table, "Eli's father was a U.S. Congressman. He's very interested in politics himself. With your political science background, you two should have a lot in common."

A blush burned Evie's cheeks. Could her father be more blatant? "I really don't have much of a background. I'm just now getting into the real poly sci courses," she explained.

"Oh, that's okay," Eli excused her. "Dad never played much by the established rules—you know, you scratch my back, I'll scratch yours. He was more of a wild card. He believed he was sent to Washington to represent the voters, and he would do whatever they needed."

"He made certain we got the same amount of money other states received." Evie's father laughed. "I sure have missed him these last couple of years."

"Me, too," Eli whispered.

Evie noted the sadness in his voice and shot a questioning gaze at her father.

"Congressman Wheatly suffered a heart attack during his last re-election campaign and passed away several weeks later," her father explained. "You surely remember seeing it on the news, Evie."

Evie nodded, searching her memories of political news for something about an ill congressman. Maybe she did remember that story during her freshman year, but she'd been so busy studying and pledging her sorority that she had paid little attention to the national and state news that year.

Her father continued his match-making quest despite Evie's

obvious silence, "Evie, here, wants to be a campaign manager when she graduates," her father said, beaming a smile toward their guest.

Evie responded with a polite smile of her own.

"Really?" Eli's voice filled with interest over this latest bit of information. "Are you more interested in a state campaign or something more on a national level?"

Evie knew her smile could not last forever, so she plunged into the conversation, swearing silently to have a word with her parents when Eli left. "I think I'd like to start out with a state race, maybe a local representative or senator, and then, if someone worthy runs, I'd love to work on the governor's campaign. Eventually I want to get involved with a national campaign, but I want to do more than hand out buttons and answer phones. I want to be involved in the policy making. To do that, I need to get my feet wet."

Eli nodded as Evie spoke, his brown eyes alive with true interest. He seemed to be really processing her statements, not simply nodding in agreement out of politeness. "Sounds like you have a well-thought-out plan in mind," he encouraged her.

"So how long do you plan to wait before you campaign for your father's seat?" Evie's father asked, turning the conversation to Eli.

"I'm a bit like Evie. I think I need to get my feet wet. No one here knows me except by my father's name, and I want to make a name for myself. While I admired my father and many of his positions, we disagreed about many issues. I wouldn't want people to vote for me, expecting to get my father, and then be disappointed."

Two hours later Evie's mind reeled from the avid political discussion. She used her fork to gracefully scrape the remaining chocolate icing from her dessert plate and swallowed her last sip of coffee. She forced herself to yawn and looked pointedly at her mother and then to Eli and her father.

When the conversation lulled, she spoke up. "Eli, it was nice meeting you, but I really do need to excuse myself. I have mid-terms next week and need to get a head start studying."

Eli nodded in her direction, his mouth filled with a bite of chocolate cake.

"Mother," she added as she stood and turned toward her mother, "dinner was wonderful."

She stopped on her way out of the room and planted a kiss on her mother's head. From the doorway she turned and gave Taylor and Leigh Anna a slight wave and smiled at the sight of their eyes wide with shock at her sudden departure.

Once Evie escaped the dining room, she hurried upstairs to her room, her sandals making a dull thud on the stairs as she almost skipped up them. Her heart pounded as she closed the door behind her. Before she thought about tackling her heavy backpack, she picked up her cell phone and checked for messages. Her heart sank when she saw no missed calls. She had to figure out what she would tell Ben before she talked to him, but in her heart she longed to at least know he was thinking about her.

She stared out the window at her BMW convertible, a high school graduation present from her parents. Her brother's Escalade and a jet black Lincoln sedan she did not recognize but presumed belonged to their guest were also in the driveway. In the middle of the drive a large fountain bubbled, the water sparkling from the floodlights inside it.

Beyond their home lay farmland that had belonged to her family for centuries. Normally, she loved it. But tonight, the wide expanse of land and dark sky twinkling with stars made her room feel claustrophobic.

Evie rummaged through her backpack until she found her notes from her news writing class. With notes in hand, she picked up a green chenille throw from her bed and stuck a pen behind her ear. She opened her door, careful not to let it squeak, and listened for a moment.

No voices.

After venturing into the hallway, she paused again before easing down the stairs. She didn't want anyone to catch her sneaking around. Muted voices now filtered into the foyer from the dining room, so she hurried down the last few steps. Silently opening the door to the front porch, she slipped into the cool September night.

Evie slid off her sandals and sat in the large white swing, tucking her feet under her and the throw around her. Propping her notebook in her lap, she began to read. But thoughts of Ben and the decision before her continued to return, distracting her from her notes. Finally, she decided that, if she allowed herself to focus on the problem, she'd only grow more angry—an emotion she didn't need, especially right now.

Evie lost track of time as she filled her mind instead with the notes in front of her.

She jumped when the front door opened a couple of hours later.

"It was nice to see you again, Thomas," Eli said, his back to Evie as he extended a hand to shake her father's. "Dinner was wonderful. Thank you again."

Evie only heard a muffled reply from her father.

The door closed quickly behind Eli. As he turned to walk to his car, his eyes caught Evie's. "Evie…" He paused his search for his keys. "I didn't see you here."

Evie smiled in return.

Eli walked toward her. Without waiting for an invitation, he set his briefcase on the porch and settled onto the other end of the swing. "It's beautiful out here," he remarked.

Evie rolled her eyes.

"What?" he asked, as though he thought he'd missed the punch line to a joke.

"You don't get it, do you?" Evie asked in disbelief.

Eli lifted a brow. Finally, he shook his head slowly.

"You were not brought here to discuss legal matters with my parents," she explained, struggling to keep her voice quiet. "This was a date. My parents are trying to fix me up, and you're a pawn in their game."

"If what you say is true, then I'm flattered your parents consider me worthy of dating their daughter." A smile played at his lips.

"I don't need them to fix me up," she growled. "I *have* a boyfriend. They just don't approve of him. He's not from the right family."

How could someone who seemed so smart play right into her parents' hands? Could he really have had no clue?

"I see...and because my father was a congressman, and I'm a lawyer, I would make a suitable boyfriend."

"Not boyfriend," she corrected him, allowing the statement to hang in the air before finishing it. "Husband." The word cut through the flirting, leaving only silence in its place.

Evie almost regretted saying it. Almost. Eli seemed nice enough, and she hated to drop reality into his lap this way, but he had to know her parents' intentions were not innocent.

"Wow." Eli merely mouthed the word.

They sat for a minute in uncomfortable silence.

"Evie..." Eli hesitated, as though searching for the right thing to say. He drew a breath. "If I had known, I would not have come. I am very sorry your parents put you in this position. I haven't lived here in many, many years and truly looked forward to meeting some people outside the baby boomer era. But I understand your anger.

"I never dated much because the women my parents suggested were more interested in shopping, getting their nails done, and bragging about the future occupations of the men they dated. I rarely found someone who wanted to be with me for me and not for my family name. If you have found a boyfriend who fits that description, hold on to him. They are few and far between."

Evie's face burned as his words sank in. Embarrassment overtook her anger as she stared into Eli's dark, sincere eyes. "Ben is just like that," she whispered. "He doesn't care how much money I have or who my parents are. He's more comfortable eating fast food than at four-star restaurants." She thought of her boyfriend—his warm smile and brilliant blue eyes. "He asked me out before he knew who my parents were."

"Sounds like you have a good thing going," Eli commented. The swing swayed back and forth when he stood. "Well, it's time for me to get out of here. It was really nice to meet you tonight, and good luck with your mid-terms next week." He smiled down at her and then picked up his briefcase.

Evie watched Eli walk down the steps and then drive away into the night. She closed her eyes, rested her head on the back of the swing, and sighed. *Maybe Eli isn't too bad after all.* Now at least he knew where she stood so he wouldn't make excuses to drop by her parents' house when he knew she would be home. He knew she was off limits.

Yet something about that thought unsettled her. Regardless of Eli's opinion of Ben, Evie had a choice to make, and only a few days to figure out what to do....

About the Author

HILARY HAMBLIN, also the author of *The Color of Love,* has lived the ups and downs of small-town life growing up in a small town of her own in North Mississippi. She has a degree in journalism, has served as Executive Director of the Baldwyn Area Chamber of Commerce, has been a summer missionary, and works as an independent marketing and advertising consultant with her own firm, Momentum Consulting, in addition to being a mom. Hilary has also published articles in *HomeLife* magazine, *Northeast Mississippi Daily Journal, The Baldwyn News,* and the e-zine *Women Today Magazine.*

www.oaktara.com